BLACK SUNDAY

Evan McHugh

An Omnibus Book from Scholastic Australia

Teachers' notes for *Black Sunday* are available from
www.scholastic.com.au

Omnibus Books
an imprint of Scholastic Australia Pty Ltd (ABN 11 000 614 577)
PO Box 579, Gosford NSW 2250.
www.scholastic.com.au

Part of the Scholastic Group
Sydney • Auckland • New York • Toronto • London • Mexico City
• New Delhi • Hong Kong • Buenos Aires • Puerto Rico

First published in 2016.
Text copyright © Evan McHugh, 2016.
Cover design copyright © Design by Committee, 2016.
The moral rights of Evan McHugh have been asserted.

ISBN 978 1 74362 799 0 (paperback)

 A catalogue record for this
book is available from the
National Library of Australia

Typeset in Minion 12pt/18pt.

Printed by McPherson's Printing Group, Maryborough, VIC.

Scholastic Australia's policy, in association with McPherson's
Printing Group, is to use papers that are renewable and made
efficiently from wood grown in responsibly managed sources,
so as to minimise its environmental footprint.

 The paper in this book is FSC® certified.
FSC® promotes environmentally responsible,
socially beneficial and economically viable
management of the world's forests.

21 22 23 24 25 / 2

Bondi,
New South Wales

1937–38

A Note about Currency, Weights and Measures

In 1937–38, Australian currency comprised pounds, shilling and pence. There were twenty shillings to a pound and twelve pence to a shilling. One pound then would be worth eighty-five dollars in today's currency, a shilling would be four dollars and twenty-five cents, and one penny would be thirty-five cents.

Australians used the Imperial system of weights and measurement. There were three feet to a yard and one foot measured thirty centimetres. A metre is slightly longer than a yard. A ton is fairly closely equal to a tonne.

Thursday, 3 June 1937

A diary! What a waste of time. Mrs Kearsley, that's my teacher, reckons a daily diary is a way to 'record the significant events in our young lives'. Really? Homework every day until the end of the year, that's what it is. Is she allowed to do that? As for significant events, I'm twelve. Nothing ever happens to me. I'm just an average kid. I've got a mum and a dad, an older brother and a little sister. I go to school, the milk bar, and the beach. Bondi, just down the hill. The only difference is when there's no school – then it's just the milk bar and the beach. That's the whole story of my life.

The other thing Mrs Kearsley says you can do in a diary is write down your dreams and aspirations. That's even easier. I want to be a Bondi lifesaver like Grampa Jack. So, that's my life story done. I'm goin' down the beach.

Thursday, 17 June 1937

Okay, so now I've got something to write about. I had a big fight with my teacher. A really big fight. About the diary. Two weeks after she'd got us to start writing the thing, she told us to bring it in so she could see what we'd written. I'm not joking! Plenty of kids got into trouble because they hadn't written anything, and I thought I'd get an earbashing because I'd only written in it once. Not that I cared. Even if Mrs Kearsley gave me the cane, I reckon I wouldn't blink. But it was when she reached for my exercise book that, all of sudden, I didn't want her to see it. I was almost as surprised as she was.

'David McCutcheon, stop playing the fool and show me your work,' she said with that snooty voice she puts on with the dumb kids in class.

'No,' I said. And I was holding on to the book really tight. Then I mumbled, 'It's private.'

She laughed at me, and my face started going red. I was real embarrassed but a bit angry too. 'You stupid boy,' she said. 'Nothing you write could possibly be of interest to me, but I will see that you've done what was asked.'

She started to reach for the book again but I wasn't having it. The whole classroom was completely silent. Everyone was staring. Part of me just wanted to show her the book and get it over with. But I just couldn't do it.

'No,' I said again. Even as the word came out I knew I was getting in hot water, but I really meant it. I reckon

I'd have fought Les Darcy (the best boxer who ever lived, according to Grampa Jack) before I gave in. Sure enough, that just made things worse. She stopped reaching for the book but I could see Mrs Kearsley getting real curious about what I had to hide.

Then she said, 'Typical McCutcheon. If you keep on like this you'll end up like your brother.'

That's when I lost my temper. Jamie left school as soon as he was old enough. Mrs Kearsley was a big part of the reason why. He hated school in general but her in particular. I still reckon it's her fault he got sent away to the country. So I said something to her that's so bad I can't even write it in here, plus a lot of swear words, and I've never seen anyone get so angry. She sent me to the principal. When Mr Kerr found out what I had said, he looked like he was going to explode. His hands were actually shaking. He grabbed me by the ear and twisted me round. He hung on to my ear the whole time he walked me out of the school, down the road and all the way through Bondi to my place.

'There's been an incident at the school,' he said to Mum when she came to the door. He didn't let go of my ear until we were in the sitting room. Us kids are only allowed in there to listen to the wireless, and have to be on our best behaviour. I couldn't help thinking this was going to go the whole fifteen rounds.

Mr Kerr told Mum I'd used abusive language to my teacher and that 'under the circumstances, David's future at the school may be untenable'. I think he meant I was going to be expelled. That's when Mum told me to go to my room (well, the sleepout where I've got my bed and Jamie used to have his). Mr Kerr eventually left and Mum came and said, 'Do not set foot out of this room until your father gets home.'

I've been here ever since. I've missed walking Grampa Jack home from the Diggers, which is where he goes for a couple of beers after work with his old war mates. I do that every day now that Jamie has gone to work on Uncle Neville and Auntie May's dairy farm. Reckon I might be joining him there when Dad gets home. I'm really gonna cop it. It'll be on for young and old, as Grampa Jack says. But I know for sure no one will bother to find out my side of the story. Turns out this diary is about the only thing that'll listen to a kid like me.

Thursday, 24 June 1937

I knew it. Mum and Dad didn't even ask what happened. When he came home, Dad didn't get mad. He just said, 'You *will* apologise to Mrs Kearsley and hope for your own sake that the school will take you back.' Then Grampa Jack came in to say g'day. He'd heard about what happened, even down at the Diggers, and realised I wouldn't be coming to walk home with him like I usually do.

He just said, 'Nipper (that's my nickname), Mrs Kearsley is a good woman and you've done wrong by her. You shouldn't have called her a dried-up old cow.'

When I tried to argue he just said, 'It's good that you stood up for yourself. But have you stood up for what's right?'

So the next day, at lunchtime, Mum took me back to school and we went to the principal's office. Mr Kerr and Mrs Kearsley were waiting.

I said, 'I'm really sorry for what I said. It won't happen again.'

Then Mrs Kearsley said, 'I accept your apology. You may return to my class.'

Now part of me wishes I got kicked out of school.

Mrs Kearsley might have accepted my apology, but I reckon she hasn't forgiven me. She hates me as much as she hated Jamie. But you know what? She's stopped asking to look at our diaries. Mine especially. And not just because I don't take it anywhere near school.

Sunday, 27 June 1937

Hey diary. I'm not writing in you today because Mrs Kearsley says so but because today was perfect. So I thought I'd write it down so I wouldn't forget it. Summer's the best time of the year at Bondi, especially when there's school holidays, but some of my favourite days are in winter. There's almost no people at the beach, just the locals, and when it's warm and sunny you can still go swimming and there's no crowds. You've almost got the waves to yourself.

They call the people who swim in the ocean baths 'Icebergs' because they swim all year round, but it's really not that cold yet. Today was still warm enough to swim. The sea was blue as blue and almost smooth 'cause there was no wind. There was just a bit of a swell from some storm far away in the ocean and it was rolling over into perfect little green waves. And the water was crystal clear. Grampa Jack was down training with the other lifesavers and my best mate Damo and all the kids in our gang were swimming right out the back so they could 'rescue' us. I got 'saved' three times.

When Grampa Jack's crew were done they left the surf reel on the beach so us kids could practise rescuing each other. It's so easy I reckon they should let us big kids (boys and girls) be lifesavers now. But it's the same old story: 'You're too young.' And of course girls aren't allowed to be lifesavers. Dunno why. Even Mum and Dad came down and later they treated me and Josie (that's my little sister, who used to be a pest until I realised she looks up to me like I look up to Jamie) to fish and chips from the Greeks'. Like I said, a perfect day.

Tuesday, 29 June 1937

Gee, I get in trouble a lot. Today, trouble again. I got caught nicking an apple from the greengrocer's. And the bloke told Grampa Jack. Next thing you know it was like I'd robbed the Bank of England. Or worse still, the bank where Dad works. Grampa Jack said he'd put me over his knee but I was getting too big. I'm almost as tall as Grampa Jack but nowhere near as strong. It was all 'you're dragging the McCutcheon name through the mud', 'you're no better than a common thief' and on and on. Lucky he didn't find out I was wagging the last bit of school with Damo when it happened. As usual, Damo was too smart to get caught. But me?

Grampa Jack told Mum, and Mum just pointed at the bowl of fruit in the kitchen. 'If you want fruit, there's plenty there,' she said.

How can you explain it's not the same? Dunno why, but apples always taste better when you knick 'em with your mates. And it's only apples. Anyway, it was the usual 'go to the sleepout and reflect on the error of your ways until Dad gets home'. Actually it's kind of convenient because it means I've got time to write about all me troubles. Well, there's nothin' better to do. The beach today was like a pond. No waves except these little things flopping over on the edge of the sand. You could have launched Grampa Jack's rowboat, no worries.

Wednesday, 30 June 1937

Hey diary. Today I've been making amends. For Dad and Mr Smith, the greengrocer. Dad was really angry when he found out about the apple, but not in the usual way. Turns out Mr Smith is a customer of Dad's bank and Dad reckons it looks really bad if his son gets caught robbing a customer. Well, even I could see that once he explained it, which he did with that voice he has when he's talking about bank business. I usually can't make any sense of what he's saying but I did this time. Anyway, he took me around to Mr Smith and to make it up to him I had to help after school for a week, doing deliveries around the neighbourhood. And I have to call him Mr Smith even though everyone else calls him Bob, or Bob the Grocer. I got through the deliveries quick as I could 'cause I still wanted to walk Grampa home from the Diggers at the usual time, so Mr Smith was pretty impressed. He reckoned I was the best delivery boy he'd ever had. He even wanted to give me a couple of pennies but Dad had already said that was no go.

So Mr Smith laughed and said, 'Righto, how about an apple? You've earned it.'

Know what? Tasted beaut.

The surf came back from its holiday today. Regular breakers, like they'd never been gone.

Wednesday, 7 July 1937

Today I did something good for a change. I'd been reading over what I'd written in here, and I was feeling pretty proud that I'd written so much. It's already more than I've ever written in my life. Trouble was, I wasn't so proud of some of the things I've done. I don't reckon I'm that bad, even if people like Mrs Kearsley think otherwise, but when it's there in black and white (or blue, actually) and you wrote it yourself, it's hard to argue. Anyway, I was trying to work out how to prove it when I came to the end of my week helping Mr Smith.

He said, 'Thanks, you've been a real help.'

And then it struck me. I knew what to do. So I said, 'I'll see you tomorrow, Mr Smith.'

He looked a bit confused because he knew Dad said I only had to help him for a week. So I explained.

'This week was because Mum and Dad made me do it,' I said. 'Next week is so you know I'm sorry.'

Mr Smith got a real funny look on his face and then he smiled.

'She's apples,' he said.

That's greengrocer talk for yes. I didn't say it was also because Mr Smith is a good bloke and I like helping him, but I reckon he probably knows.

The other thing I noticed in here was about the fight I had with Mrs Kearsley. When I read it over I couldn't remember what was so private in my first entry that I didn't want her to see. Then I realised it was the thing about being a lifesaver. I dunno if I can explain why, but I know I want to be a lifesaver more than anything. When you see Grampa Jack, who's a paid beach inspector and a volunteer lifesaver, and his mates saving someone, it's just the best thing. Everyone's panicking except them. Then you see them at surf carnivals marching past in perfect step, heads back, solid as a rock. They're just the best.

The thing is, when I think about being a lifesaver, the first thing that pops into my head is 'You'll never be good enough'. I'd just hate it if someone, anyone, ever said that to me. I reckon that's what Mrs Kearsley would have done. She'd have said out loud what I'm afraid of all the time. What if I'm not good enough?

The beach was all churned up today. There must be a big storm out to sea somewhere, as the swell was building all day. By the afternoon the waves were breaking right out past Ben Buckler, that's on the north headland, near the flat where we live. The combers were foaming all the way into the beach and there was froth everywhere. Grampa Jack reckons we might be in for a big blow.

Thursday, 8 July 1937

Gee, don't word travel fast. Mum and Dad found out about what I did for Mr Smith 'cause Mum shops there. So she found out, and Dad found out, and well, talk about being in their good books.

Mum says, 'I think you showed your true character.'

Then Dad goes, 'Proud of you, son.'

Only Josie went, 'It's just vegies.'

Saturday, 10 July 1937

What a storm! Two whole days of wind and rain and raging seas. I wish I could write better so I could describe it. Or the way Grampa Jack did. He said, 'Looks like King

Neptune has sent his water giants into battle against his mortal enemy, the land.' It was just like that. The first attack had already begun when dawn broke on Friday morning. The whole coastline was battered by enormous boiling surf that seemed to grow bigger by the hour. The tops of the breakers were being torn away by the wind and the spray was flung up the faces of the cliffs. The headlands had stopped looking like ordinary blocks of yellow stone and had become battlements of some giant castle trying to stand firm against the thundering attacks from the sea. Sometimes the clash between wave and stone was so violent that the ground shook. We could feel the thump and rumble at school all through the day. No one could concentrate, not even Mrs Kearsley, so she gave us a bit of a lesson on the weather.

She told us that storms like the one we're having are called an East Coast Low, a low-pressure system that gets more intense once it gets over the sea. They can hit the east coast of Australia from Tasmania to Queensland at any time of the year. Further north, they call such storms cyclones or hurricanes, and they may be even bigger because they're in the tropics. But an East Coast Low can sometimes match them, and they've long been feared by sailors, owing to the danger of being shipwrecked. She said there were lots of wrecks on our piece of coast including the *Dunbar*, just between Bondi and the entrance to Sydney Harbour. And then there's the *Malabar* (which ran aground in fog in 1931) and the *Hereward* at Maroubra (in 1898), both south of Bondi.

After school was over I went straight home. It was too wild to be outside doing deliveries for Mr Smith or walking Grampa Jack home. We can usually see the beach from the front windows of our block of flats, but the spray was so bad that we couldn't see the front yard.

I hadn't been home long when Grampa Jack came and got me.

'Come on, Nip,' he said, 'you don't want to miss this.'

He started pulling out a raincoat and sou'wester for me while Mum raised a fuss.

'He'll be soaked through,' she argued. 'He'll end up with pneumonia.'

I didn't want to admit it, but I was on Mum's side. Grampa Jack just winked.

'Did *you* catch your death when I took you out when you were just a lass?' he asked. 'You used to pester me to go, remember? You loved it.'

That stopped her. She looked at Grampa Jack, then she looked at me. 'Ben Buckler,' she said. 'Right out on the end. That's the best place. For two pins I'd come with you.'

She bundled me up in several layers of warm clothes, then covered me in smelly rubber rainproofs and gumboots and pushed a sou'wester down hard on me head. I could hardly move. Of course Josie wanted to come, but Grampa Jack said she could go with him when the next big storm came. When Grampa Jack and I left, Mum was trying to clean a little space on a window so she could look out herself.

Up on Ben Buckler, the ocean was unlike anything I'd ever seen. It was late afternoon but there was a strange kind of grey-blue darkness all along the coast. Then out of the murk and wind-blown rain and spray, beneath the low, dark scudding clouds, the great waves came. Line after line of them, the colour of lead and stone, like mountains with deep valleys in between, rolling towards the land, then rising higher until they toppled over, deep green in colour, and broke with a crashing roar of white foam and spray. From on top of the cliffs we could feel the shock of each wave as it slammed against the rocks and threw fountains of water into the air, where the wind snatched it up and blew it with such force that it sprayed in a continuous stream over the place where we were standing. Below, the wave spent its force and fell back into a surge of broken, churning water. As far as we could see, to the north and south, the entire ocean was in constant rolling, breaking, heaving motion.

Believe it or not, we weren't alone. There were at least a hundred people up there enjoying the spectacle or 'braving the elements' as some put it. And despite the driving rain and wind, more people were coming than were going away.

While we were there, Grampa Jack told me about the storm that threw up a giant rock when he was younger. 'It was before the war,' he told me. 'Around 1912, I think. You see that big rock there? That's the one. It weighs more than two hundred tons, and the ocean had no trouble moving it. No trouble at all.'

'Did anyone see it?'

'No, it happened at night. We just woke up one morning and it was there.'

Then I said, 'You wouldn't want to rescue someone when the ocean was like this.'

'I dunno, young fella,' Grampa Jack said. 'We once went out when it was nearly this bad. There was one of them beachcombers, like Southerly Jack, and those other fellas over there on the beach. See how they go along right where the waves are washing up the sand, looking for coins and wedding rings? It was a day like this, winter, 'bout ten, fifteen years ago. This bloke got greedy, or saw something special, and went in to his waist. Didn't see the wave that got him. Before he knew it he was sucked out on the backwash. Couldn't swim.

'So here's me and my mate Percy – you know, Percy Lawler. He's another beach inspector. We were the only ones that saw him go in. The beach was closed. No reels, no one on duty. And we went after him. Stripped to our underwear and swam out and got him.'

He made it sound simple, but I'm sure it wasn't.

'Did everyone make a fuss?' I asked.

'Nah,' Grampa Jack said. 'Never told anyone. And the bloke wasn't so grateful. He was gonna drown but he was more upset that he'd lost whatever it was he'd found. And your gran, she was alive then, God rest her, she just gave me the rounds of the kitchen for goin' swimmin' in winter. Never asked me why.'

'But you were a hero. You might have got an award for bravery.'

Grampa just stared at the ocean for a while after I said that, like he was remembering something. Then he shook his head and said, 'Most heroes I've met dunno much about bravery.'

Then he grinned at me. 'Come on, young Nipper. Better get you home before you get so wet your mum thinks *you've* been swimmin.'

Monday, 12 July 1937

Hey diary. There's supposed to be a calm before the storm, but this time it was the other way around. First the storm, then the calm. Today the sun was shining. There wasn't a cloud to be seen and there was barely a wave on the shore. It was like the sea was exhausted from all its tossing and churning.

The beach was swept clean, and even all Bondi feels different now. In the middle of winter people have stopped coming to the beach from all around and the only people are the ones who live here. You know nearly everyone you see. It's like a little village. I'm not sure which way I prefer. It's strange when it's so deserted, especially when you know what it's like when there are so many people around.

As usual, I walked home with Grampa Jack from the Diggers. We walked along the beach while he told me stories. One time he rescued a pregnant lady. Then there was the time Bea Miles, a strange woman who many people thought was a witch, came down to the beach with a lamb.

'Old Aub Laidlaw, one of the beach inspectors, told her it was no go,' said Grampa Jack. 'He pointed to a sign that said "No Dogs", but Bea told him the sign didn't apply to sheep. So Aub said, "But there's no grass for him to eat". Bea replied, "He isn't here to graze, he's here to sunbathe." Aub wasn't going to argue with her. She always carries a knife when she's at the beach. She reckons it's to fight off sharks. I reckon she needs it. She's one of those people who swims from one end of the beach to the other, out behind the breakers, from Ben Buckler to the Icebergs.'

'If she got into trouble, would anyone try to rescue her?' I asked.

'Of course,' Grampa Jack said. 'That's what lifesavers are there for.'

'What about the sharks?'

'If you were on duty, young fella, I reckon you'd be straight out there.'

'If I'm ever good enough.' I couldn't help saying it. I felt miserable just hearing the words come out.

Grampa put his hand on my shoulder and said, 'As soon as you're old enough, you'll be good enough.'

I hoped more than anything in the world that he'd be right, but I was only twelve. It would be nearly four years until I turned sixteen, when I could become a junior lifesaver. It might as well be forever.

'All in good time, young Nipper,' Grampa Jack said. 'All in good time.'

Wednesday, 14 July 1937

Hey diary. I've got a job. Mr Smith asked me if I'd like to do deliveries for an hour after school every day. Would I ever! He can't pay me much, just sixpence a day, but multiply that by five and I'll be the richest kid in Bondi, especially when some of his customers give me a little tip to say thank you. Maybe next year, when I turn thirteen and leave school, I'll be able to work for Mr Smith full time. Although that would mean I couldn't go up to Uncle Neville's farm and work with Jamie. So I'd have to choose. Although, just to complicate matters, when I told Mum and Dad, they said they'd thought I'd stay at school next year. Why would I do that? I mean, I won't have Mrs Kearsley to bother me any more, but if it isn't her, it'll be someone else.

Dad just said, 'You owe it to yourself to put your head down and study. Make something of your life.'

How do you explain to someone as brainy as Dad that you don't have to go to school to learn how to be a lifesaver?

The surf today was all confused. It was a bit grey and windy, and the waves were coming from about three different directions at once, all choppy and changey. While Grampa Jack and me were looking, I tried to imagine what it would be like to dive in and try and rescue someone. Even though the water was pretty rough, if I was a lifesaver, that's what I'd have to do.

Tuesday, 20 July 1937

Great news, diary. I got a letter from me brother Jamie. Well, actually, the family got a letter but Jamie put in a little bit for each of us: Mum, Dad, Grampa Jack, Josie and me. He told everyone about working at Uncle Neville and Auntie May's dairy, gettin' up before dawn to get the cows in, milking every day. This is what he wrote just to me:

Dear Nipper,

I miss you lots, little brother, and being home and going down the beach every day, but now I've got me own horse, there's plenty to keep me busy and keep me mind off things. Like, sometimes I wish I was there, but when me and a few of the local blokes go riding up in the hills, I wish you were here. There's kangaroos, and caves, and rivers for swimming (when it's warm), and no one else around. Me horse is an old mare, a broken-in brumby from the Barrington Ranges, which are some big mountains over the other side of the Hunter River. Really wild country. The mare's pretty quiet but sometimes she gets in a bit of a mood, so I've called her Mrs Kearsley, or Mrs K for short. She's only chucked me off a couple of times but now I reckon I'm getting smart to her

ways. Or she's worked out that if she goes to the trouble of
bucking me, I'm just gonna get back on.

I hear you've been getting into trouble with the real
Mrs Kearsley, but who hasn't? There's not much you can
do except wait until next year when you go to the next class
up. Of course, you could chuck school early, like I did, but I
reckon Mum and Dad won't let you. You're way better with
your books than I ever was. You're almost as smart as Dad.
So I reckon you're trapped, Nip. Mind you, that doesn't
mean you can't come up to visit next holidays. Auntie
May and Uncle Neville reckon you'd be welcome if you're
prepared to work twelve hours a day. Just kidding. Maybe.

And today's surf? Nice three-foot waves with an
offshore breeze. The water was crystal clear, but a little
bit cold for swimming. I know, 'cause I went swimming.
Got up early, everyone still asleep, and went down to see
if I could make myself go in. At first I couldn't, it was
that cold, then I imagined someone in trouble, out in the
breakers, and that helped.

Dad was up when I came home, saw me come in,
but he didn't say anything.

Friday, 23 July 1937

Getting a letter from Jamie was really good, but it also made me sad. While I was reading it, it was almost like he was back at home. I could almost hear him rather than see what he was saying. Then, when I finished reading, it was like he was suddenly gone. He was far away again. No more big brother to run to if someone picked on me. No one who knew everything and was never too busy to explain. No one who took the blame when it was my fault. Well, sometimes.

I've never got a letter before, and I never knew that when you read it, it could bring whoever it was back to you, at least for as long as you're reading it. I wonder if that's what it will be like if someone reads this diary years from now. One minute I'll be here, then they'll close the exercise book and I'll be gone. Not that they'd be likely to get this far. My life isn't that interesting. Not like Grampa Jack's. He's got lots of stories to tell. Come to think of it, everyone does.

Mum and Dad have the story of how they met, which they tell over and over. Mum was born and bred in Bondi, just like Grampa Jack, who's her dad, while Dad comes from the farm where Jamie is now, in the Hunter

Valley, that's north of Sydney. He was down in Sydney going to university (he's really, really smart) and he met Mum when he went swimming at the beach and got into trouble. He got caught in a rip and started getting swept out to sea. He was trying to swim back to the beach against the rip instead of across it, and he was starting to tire and worry about whether he was going to make it. That's when Mum reckons she rescued him, even though she's not a real lifesaver. She swam over and showed him how to swim across the current until they were out of the rip. By the time they'd made it back to the beach, Dad was so impressed, and so grateful, he asked her out. Dad still isn't a good swimmer, but Mum's like everyone else around here: part fish. She'd be a great lifesaver only of course women aren't allowed to do that. That doesn't stop her and a lot of other women getting involved in all the fundraising and organising that goes on with the club, especially when there are competitions on. And Dad still calls her his lifesaver.

As for Josie, my little sister, she's got such an imagination that stories just swirl around her. She's always going on about how this happened to her, and then that happened, or something happened to one of her friends. They're really only little things, but not to her. She's funny that way. I reckon she could write an entire book about her pigtails. She loves those things. Makes Mum braid them for her every morning before school, then flicks them around and talks endlessly about them getting longer and longer. Josie is three years younger than me, and when she was little she was always hanging around. It used to bother me until Jamie told me that's what I always did with him. When I realised that, I didn't mind so much. I actually quite like it.

Of course, the one with all the stories is Grampa Jack. He's one of the oldest members of the Bondi Life Saving Club, which is the oldest in Australia, established in 1907. He's been swimming at Bondi since even before that. He can still remember when there were rules about the times when you could swim at the beach. He was also one of the first to do his bronze medallion, just after they were introduced in 1910. Then he was one of the club's members who went to the Great War. More than half the membership went. In 1915, thirty-nine out of the club's seventy-seven members were enlisted. Two of them, Jack Barlow and Robert Crowe, landed at Gallipoli on 25 April. Neither of them survived long. Robert was killed eight days later. Jack was killed in August.

Grampa Jack was almost too old to go. He never talks about what happened in the war, but I do know that he was given a medal for doing something brave. He won't say what. The only thing I've ever heard him say about it was, 'I was thirty-four when the war started and they wouldn't have me. But after a couple of years they'd lost so many that they'd take anyone. By then they'd realised they couldn't throw away people's lives like they'd been doing. Reckon that's the only thing that got us through.'

The water at the beach today was like glass, with waves rising up like whales, all smooth-backed until they broke and rolled, slowly foaming, to the shore. A couple of blokes from the surf club were out surfing. Saw this old lady called Bondi Mary scavenging along the shore as well.

Sunday, 25 July 1937

It's the middle of winter and today was just too cold to go in the water, so me and Damo went over and watched the Icebergs. What are Icebergs? Over on the southern end of Bondi, there's this swimming club that swims all year round. Even though it's freezing, they're still swimming. Some swim every day, but most swim on weekends, when they have time. Because they swim when the water is really cold, they've called themselves the Bondi Icebergs. They started out in 1929 and everyone thought they were mad and it wouldn't last, but eight years later they're still going. They have a big ceremony at the beginning of winter but they keep on going right through the cold months.

It was a sunny day, but Damo wasn't even tempted to jump in. We just watched these older men and women dive in and shiver their way up and down the pool, swimming lengths like it was perfectly fine. They reckon once you get moving it's not so cold but I don't reckon it's true. That's because I've been swimming three times this week. Early morning. Dive in, out through the breakers, then back. It's really cold when you get in, and it's still really cold when you get out.

I didn't mention that to Damo, even though he's my best mate. Don't want him to laugh at me. I can't explain why. Well, actually, I can. I just don't want to put it into words.

Grampa Jack isn't an Iceberg. He reckons the only

way he'll go in when it's cold is if someone is drowning. Of course, if the weather's fine, he'll have a swim in the surf, but that's not being an Iceberg, that's just enjoying Bondi.

I haven't explained about Damo much, but we've been best friends for as long as we can remember. He lives just two doors down from us. His mum and my mum have been taking us down to the beach together since we were babies, and we learned to swim together. Damo is so smart that he never gets into trouble, and he's got this way about him that even when he does do the wrong thing, people don't seem to mind much. For example, Mrs Kearsley knows he's my best mate but she still likes him.

'It's me smile,' he reckons. 'Flash 'em your pearly whites and look innocent. That's the secret.'

I know what he means. When he smiles or laughs, you can't help but do the same. He reckons when I've done the wrong thing, it's written all over my face. Sometimes I think it must be in capital letters: *GUILTY*.

There's lots of other kids we hang around with, because we all go down to the beach together. If we're goin' out to see what's happening, Damo and me always pick each other up on the way. About the only time we don't go anywhere together is when I go fishin' with Grampa Jack, and when I walk home with Grampa Jack from the Diggers. Damo could come fishin', but he doesn't like going out in the dinghy. That, and the dinghy doesn't have enough room for three. He might be scared of going on the water, but he's afraid of nothing when it comes to going in it. He'll dive off the rocks into the waves. He'll catch dumpers if there's nothing else. And he never gets hurt, or if he does, he doesn't seem to mind.

Thursday, 29 July 1937

There's lots of excitement in Ramsgate Avenue today. A new family moved into the flat next door. There's a dad and mum and a girl about my age. I saw her and she saw me but I didn't say hello for some reason. Anyway, this small truck arrived after school was over and unloaded a couple of trunks of their belongings. That seemed to be all they had. The truck was only there a couple of minutes before it drove off.

Everyone was dying to know what was going on, but it wasn't hard to find out because Nosy Josie just marched in and said hello and found out that the family was Mr and Mrs Friedman (but someone had changed it to *Freeman* because it was easier to spell) and their daughter Rachel. They were from Germany and they could hardly speak any English and they had almost no furniture.

Josie kept running back and forth telling us bits of news even though it turns out Mum already knew all about them. She and Dad and Grampa Jack had something to do with them coming to Bondi. Mum kept telling Josie to leave them alone to settle in, but when Mum heard that they didn't have much stuff, she went straight over to introduce herself and find out what they needed.

Mrs Freeman told Mum she was very kind but she couldn't possibly accept anything. Of course that meant nothing to Mum and all the other people in the street. By the time everyone's dads got home, the Freemans had nearly everything they needed until they got their own. Then various dads pitched in to carry over a table the Browns hardly ever used and an old bed frame that was under someone else's house, and some mattresses to go with them.

'The only thing they need now is a radio, and maybe a piana,' Josie reckoned. 'Piano,' Mum corrected. Mum also let Mrs Freeman use our icebox to keep milk and meat and butter fresh, until they got their own.

Josie announced that Rachel was her new best friend, that even though Rachel spoke hardly any English, they could understand each other perfectly. Mum said that Josie being a chatterbox and no one else being able to say anything didn't mean they understood. That went right in one of Josie's ears and out the other.

When Dad got home, he went straight over and introduced himself to Mr Freeman. Somehow they already know each other. Not only that, but Mr Freeman is going to work at Dad's bank.

Monday, 2 August 1937

Hey diary. There's a funny thing about Bondi. Everyone thinks the Icebergs are a bit strange in the head for swimming in winter, but today is the first day of August, which means there's only one more month until summer starts. Yes, I know September is really the start of spring, but in Bondi it's different. Everyone starts swimming again, even if the water's cold and sometimes even if the weather is cold. Everyone knows that every day it will get warmer and warmer and better and better, but if you don't start swimming early, you'll miss out on the fun. I can hardly wait. Maybe that's what keeps the Icebergs going: they don't have to wait.

As soon as she got home from school, Josie went straight over to see Rachel. Josie was so eager it made me think she'd prefer to have a big sister rather than a brother like me. Rachel didn't go to school today. I think it might have been because she couldn't understand what the teachers said. How lucky is that? I can understand every nasty thing Mrs Kearsley says to me, and I can't wait for the day I don't have to put up with it any more.

Walking Grampa Jack home tonight, I mentioned the new people next door and he said, 'Yeah, I know all about them.'

'You do?'

'Of course, Nipper,' he said. 'Your dad asked me to sponsor them out here.'

Grampa Jack explained that if you're foreign you can't come to Australia unless someone sponsors you.

Dad had already sponsored some other people, and a lot of his friends had sponsored people, so he asked Grampa Jack if he'd sponsor the Freemans. He said, 'Righto.'

'I was thinking to come around to say hello,' he said. 'When they're settled in. Maybe you could introduce me.'

I didn't say anything but I started to blush.

Grampa Jack gave me a funny look and said, 'You could introduce me to their daughter too. I think she's about your age.'

I blushed even more.

'You right there, Nip?' Grampa Jack asked with a laugh.

'Yes, Grampa,' I said, and fortunately he changed the subject. Little secret, diary. Rachel's got really nice eyes, and she smiles when she sees me, but that just makes me feel really awkward, so I haven't even said hello.

We talked about the waves. About which, of course, Grampa Jack knows everything. 'Big storm far out,' he said, looking at the big rollers lining up from well out to sea, then coming in and breaking clean across the bay. 'See how evenly they come, and how far apart? When they're really steady like that, it means there's bad weather but it's far, far away.'

Sunday, 8 August 1937

It turns out it didn't matter that I was too shy to talk to Rachel. Thanks to Josie she's kind of automatically become part of our little neighbourhood gang. Damo gave her that smile of his and said, 'G'day, me name's Damo,' and I mumbled 'Hello, I'm David,' and then we all went to the pictures yesterday like we always do. David? Where'd that come from? Everyone calls me Nipper.

It didn't matter that Rachel couldn't understand everything we said to her. We found out we could mime things and she could understand that way. We mimed licking an ice cream instead of saying, 'Do you want an ice cream?' Although we couldn't work out how to mime the flavours. Then Rachel saw the sign with all the flavours and pointed and said, 'Chocolate. In German is *shokolade.*' I'm not sure that's how you spell it but it was almost the same in both languages.

Josie has appointed herself Rachel's official interpreter. She wasn't much help until Rachel said, 'Please, speak slowly.'

We were all surprised when Josie actually did what Rachel asked. So we all tried it. 'Josie, please speak more slowly.' No luck. She only spoke slowly to Rachel.

Grampa Jack came over on the weekend too and welcomed the Freemans to Australia. Mum and Dad were there and there was a lot of handshaking.

Mr Freeman even bowed to Grampa Jack and Dad. I think it was a German custom.

Grampa stayed to tea that night and he only embarrassed me once. He said, 'That Rachel is very pretty, don't you think, young Nip?'

I thought she was, but I couldn't say anything. I blushed and looked at the table. Mum saved me. 'Don't tease him,' she said.

Grampa didn't get a chance because Josie demanded to know who was the prettiest, her or Rachel. 'You're the prettiest McCutcheon,' Dad said, but he was looking at Mum. 'And that's saying a lot.'

Later I heard Dad and Grampa Jack talking about the Freemans. 'Things must be bad for someone of his standing to leave Germany,' Dad said.

'Is he so important?' Grampa Jack asked.

'The head of the bank came down personally to welcome him,' Dad said. 'Some government people have already invited him to lunch.'

'That sounds pretty good.'

'It's very good, believe me,' Dad said. 'But I worry what it means when people like the Freemans have to leave their home and move to the other side of the world.'

'Well, hopefully nothing bad will happen to him or his family now,' Grampa Jack said.

I didn't really understand what they were talking about, but I thought I should write it in here anyhow. Maybe I'll understand it later.

The beach today was sparkling and clean. There was a small shore break, and you could see schools of little fish lifting in the waves as they broke. The seagulls were chasing them but they couldn't catch many.

I was hoping for some big swells, to practise swimming in rougher water. I reckon I can handle them. Instead, I went out and back a few times. I swam freestyle out, porpoising under the waves, then sidestroke back, with one arm, like I was rescuing someone. It might have seemed like an odd thing to do, if anyone noticed. No one did but.

Monday, 9 August 1937

Today was Rachel's first day at our school. Josie insisted

that she would take care of her but Dad and Mum told me to look out for her as well, since she was in my class. That wasn't so easy, thanks to Mrs Kearsley.

I got Sean Sullivan, who usually sits next to me because Mrs Kearsley won't let Damo sit there, to move so Rachel and I could sit together. After she was introduced to class and Rachel sat down, Mrs Kearsley saw where she was and tried to get her to move.

She said, 'Sitting next to a McCutcheon won't get you off to a good start,' and pointed to a seat near the front.

Rachel looked at Mrs Kearsley for a moment, not really understanding what she was saying. But she saw Mrs Kearsley pointing and then she shook her head. 'David is mein friend,' she said, or something like that. And she stayed sitting next to me.

She stood up to Mrs Kearsley! On her first day!

Mrs Kearsley looked like she was going to have a fit, but she couldn't argue because Rachel couldn't understand her. And even if she did, I felt like Rachel might win.

At lunchtime the whole school wanted to sit next to Rachel. Everyone was amazed that she couldn't understand anything anyone said. All the girls from my class wanted to be her best friend, but little Josie was glued to her side.

'She only understands me,' she kept saying, while everyone was trying to teach her how to say their names and 'lunch' and 'bench' and 'asphalt' and any other things they could think of. The only time everyone stopped talking was when Rachel unwrapped her sandwiches. Chocolate! I mean slices of normal bread but instead of vegemite or jam or something, there was chocolate. We all thought she must be rich. I mean, a lot of kids at Bondi Public sometimes didn't even have lunch. Sometimes they didn't have shoes. When everyone kept begging to try her sandwiches, she ended up swapping them with other kids for things she'd never eaten before.

When it was time to play, she stayed with the girls while us boys played footy. I bagsed being Viv Thicknesse, captain of the mighty Easts, who had just won the premiership for the third year in a row, although it was a short season because the best players had to go on a ship for the Kangaroo tour to England. When I scored a try, I looked over to see if Rachel was watching, but she was learning how to say 'bubblers' or something.

After school, Josie, Damo and I got Rachel to ourselves when we walked home. Then I had to do my fruit deliveries and pick up Grampa Jack. Gee, life is getting really busy.

Grampa Jack listened while I talked about Rachel for a while. I was saying how much fun she was having when he interrupted me.

'Do you know why her parents left Germany, young Nipper?'

'No, Grampa Jack,' I said. 'Maybe they wanted to come to Bondi like everyone else.'

He shook his head. 'They were afraid of what might happen if they stayed where they were.'

'Well, they should be safe now. They're on the other side of the world,' I said.

'I really hope so,' Grampa Jack said, and his voice sounded funny, like he wasn't really sure.

We looked at the waves, like we always do. But Grampa Jack didn't have anything to say about them. I'm not sure he was really looking at them. Not that they were all that special today. Sometimes they're just waves.

Friday, 13 August 1937

Rachel and her parents have only been here a couple of weeks and it feels like they've been here forever. Mrs Freeman and Mum are best friends. My dad and Rachel's dad keep having these long conversations about bank stuff that don't seem to be in English or German. Whatever it is, no one can understand them, but that's nothing new.

As for Rachel, she is just part of our gang, and she's learning English so fast it's easy to forget she can't understand everything we say. Every morning she says, very carefully, 'Good morning, David. Good morning, Josie. Thank you for walking me to school.' Except she says 'shool' instead of school. She knows my nickname is *Nipper*, but for some reason she always calls me by my real name. She never calls Damo *Damian*.

Sunday, 15 August 1937

Rachel still can't believe us kids are allowed to go wherever we want without someone taking us. She says, 'In my country, I have nanny. We go to park.' I think a nanny was someone who looked after her when her parents weren't around. Now she does everything with us. Yesterday, like all us kids, she was given ninepence to go to the pictures: sixpence to get in, and threepence for lollies. Take note, diary: I don't get ninepence any more because I'm a 'working man' according to Dad. I have to pay for myself, which I actually quite like. Anyway, today there was a *Popeye* cartoon and the *Ace Drummond* serial, but it was hard to explain to Rachel what was going on there. Ace is an American and can fly as well as Charles Kingsford Smith who, as everyone knows, was one of the first people rescued by the Bondi lifesavers, but when he was young. Anyway, Ace has been sent to Mongolia where an evil villain named 'The Dragon' is trying to stop an airport being built. And the Dragon may be behind the disappearance of an archaeologist whose daughter is trying to find him. Then there was a newsreel, something about a war in Spain and houses being bombed, then there were the movies. It was great.

Afterwards we went down the beach and Rachel couldn't believe it when she saw the Icebergs swimming. Although in Germany, in winter, she reckons there'd be snow everywhere. At Bondi in winter it can be sunny and warm.

Today Mum and Mrs Freeman put on lunch for both our families. Mum put out all the usual things, but Mrs Freeman had all kinds of things us kids had never seen. Even the devon looked and tasted funny. At the beginning of lunch, Dad made a little speech and held up a glass of lemonade. 'Welcome to Australia,' he said, and Mr Freeman stood up and made a little bow. It made Mum and Dad blush.

That night I heard Dad talking to Mum.

'They're very nice people,' Mum was saying. 'It's hard to imagine the terrible things that have happened to them.'

'From what Mr Freeman says,' Dad said, 'they're going to get worse.'

There was a long silence and then Mum said, 'Do you think there might be another war?'

'Mr Freeman thinks so.'

There was another long silence, then Mum said, 'Jamie is fourteen. Davey's twelve.'

And Dad said, 'I think of that every time I read a newspaper.'

Now I'm confused. What has my age got to do with there being a war?

Friday, 20 August 1937

I've been doing some maths. Summer is going to be late this year. It should be next weekend but Sunday will only be 29 August. So summer, I mean Bondi summer, when we can start swimming no matter how cold it is, won't start properly until the weekend after. It's not fair, but there's nothing to be done about it except maybe count the sleeps like Josie does.

I've also been doing some maths with Grampa Jack. After hearing Mum and Dad talk about how old Jamie and I were, I asked him what difference that would make if there was a war. First Grampa Jack told me not to worry about it and kept looking at the waves breaking on the beach: dumpers, not good for swimming. Then he saw that I really wanted to know. So he explained.

'If a war starts tomorrow and it lasts as long as the last one, that's four years. So in four years, Jamie will be eighteen and you'll be sixteen. Jamie might already be old enough to go, but if there's a war starting in a year or two, there's a danger you could both be involved.'

'I don't mind a bit of danger, Grampa Jack,' I said. 'You went to the war, and everyone is proud of you.'

Grampa Jack just growled and turned away. He didn't

say anything until we'd reached the front gate of his little cottage. He stopped before going in and said, 'No one else should have to go through what we went through.'

You know, diary, Grampa Jack has this way about him. You can ask him anything – he knows just about everything – but every now and then he just clams up. It's like there's this door. It's always closed and he'll never tell what's behind it.

Anyway, after talking to Grampa Jack, I went home and did some more calculating. I turn thirteen in March 1938, fourteen in March 1939. You've got to be eighteen to go in the army, so if Australia gets into a war that lasts four years any time before then, I'll miss out. But after what Dad said, I've been starting to look at the newspaper. There's already a war in Spain, and another in China, but they've got nothing to do with Australia. There'd have to be a war with Germany, or someone like that, for us to be involved. And that doesn't seem very likely.

Sunday, 22 August 1937

One sure sign summer is just around the corner is the working bees at the surf clubs. Bondi has two: Bondi and

North Bondi. Even though we're North Bondi swimmers, Mum and Dad went down to give Grampa Jack and the other Bondi members a hand with all the little jobs that have to be done to get ready for the new season: maintenance to the reels, checking belts and lines, and making sure the club flag is looking immaculate for the march pasts in the surf carnivals. It's a pity the same can't be said for the club's surf boat. It's a bit of a wreck, but the club doesn't have the funds to buy a new one. So they patch it up, and patch it up, to keep it going. Meanwhile, Mum and the other mums reckon they're going to push even harder this year with their fundraising.

Tuesday, 24 August 1937

Rachel is already really good at school. We had a maths test today and she got the best mark in class. She's still catching up with her English, but she's already good at working out the differences between nouns and verbs and where to put apostrophes. What I like is that whenever Mrs Kearsley tells us to get out our English grammar book, *Mastering the Mother Tongue*, Rachel lets out a little snort.

Mrs Kearsley must hear her but never says anything.

It's a good thing Rachel is really smart, because she's having to learn all the time. When she's not at school, she's learning all about Bondi and being an Aussie, which is a lot of fun for us other kids. The thing is, she doesn't talk much about where she comes from. When Damo and me asked about why she had to leave she just said, 'Because of our religion.'

That doesn't seem like a very good reason. I know Rachel is Jewish, which is different from being a Christian, but then Damo is Catholic, which is different from being a Protestant, but that doesn't mean either of us has to leave Bondi. Mind you, that Adolf Hitler, the German leader, doesn't look very nice. When you see him on newsreels, he's always shouting, and thousands and thousands of people are shouting back and saluting. And he never smiles.

Great waves today. Beautiful breakers that started at one end of the beach and broke right across the bay. If it wasn't for school I could have caught waves from one end of the beach to the other.

When me and Grampa Jack went down after my grocery run, he gave me a little test.

'Righto, Nipper,' he said. 'Can you point out where the rips are?'

That was easy. Most beaches have sand banks where the waves wash in and channels where the water flows back out. The channels are called rips because if you get in one, you can end up going out to sea with the water. They're usually easy to see because the waves break cleanly on the banks but may not break at all in the rips, because the water is deeper and there's a current going against the waves. So today there was the southern rip, which is almost always there, another in the middle of the beach and another halfway between the middle and the northern end of the beach.

'Good, Nipper,' Grampa Jack said. 'Now, where would you put the flags so people can swim safely?'

I pointed out the big bank between the middle and the southern end of the beach and another bank at North Bondi where the waves are often gentler because it's a bit protected by Ben Buckler.

'Very good,' Grampa Jack said. 'We'll make a lifesaver of you yet.'

I really liked that.

Sunday, 29 August 1937

It's the last weekend of winter today, which means it's the last day when Bondi is a place where you only see the locals. Everyone is looking forward to the warmer weather, but today was a really nice day because everyone was out and about. There were people at both the lifesavers' clubs fixing things up for the start of the season. Shops and deckchair hire places were putting coats of paint on. There were even people making the bandstand near the Bondi Pavilion spick and span. Lots of other people were getting fish and chips and picnicking along the promenade or down on the sand, making the most of there not being any crowds. Us kids? Everyone went down and put their feet in the water. It was pretty cold but not so bad that you couldn't paddle and play chasings with the waves. And it was certainly warm enough that we could get ice creams when we begged for them afterwards.

Wednesday, 1 September 1937

It's the first day of spring. Only three days until summer, if you know what I mean.

Thursday, 2 September 1937

Only two days to go.

Friday, 3 September 1937

One! I'm about to go to bed, and when I wake up, it will be swimming every day now, ice creams, milkshakes and fish and chips, sunshine and sand, and surfing waves until it starts to get dark. And after that? It just gets better: school holidays. I mean the summer ones, the ones that last forever, and nothing but swimming and adventures and fun for weeks and weeks and weeks. I still like winter, but summer is the best time of all. And the beach today was like it was getting ready. The waves were smooth and clean and lining up and breaking one after the other, all very orderly. They'd roll all the way to the beach before the next one broke, then it would come rolling in, a steady endless procession of perfect waves for body surfing or surf-o-planes, or anything.

Saturday, 4 September 1937

Hey diary. At last it's summer! Yes, yes, I know it's really spring, but tell that to everyone who turned up at the beach today. It kind of makes sense. Lots of people think it's too cold to swim in winter but it's not too cold to swim in spring. And they love going for a swim. So last week there was nobody at the beach and today there were thousands of people.

Me and Josie were up as soon as it was light. Into our swimmers, then over to get Rachel and Damo, then Grampa Jack, who, first day of summer, was on the first lifesaving patrol.

We were all down on the beach just before six for our first swim. Grampa led us into the water, which was really freezing, but we went in anyway, diving under the waves and coming up whooping and cheering with that wonderful fizzy water feeling all over us.

All, that is, except Rachel, who isn't a very good swimmer. Grampa stayed with her in the shallower water and we body surfed back to them then turned and dived under the waves to get back out again.

Most of the kids from our school were there, and after a while there were lots of parents and other people coming down to the beach for their first swim. Then loads of people started getting off the trams – double trams because so many people wanted to come to Bondi – and everyone headed for the water.

Grampa Jack went on patrol and Josie, Damo and I came in closer to shore to make sure Rachel was okay. Then we got out of the water and sat up on the beach until Mum and Dad and Rachel's and Damo's parents came down. When they did, we went straight back in.

Rachel noticed that there were signs on the beach in German telling her to bathe between the flags. The signs were in German and Italian, to help visitors who didn't speak English. We explained to Rachel that the safest place to swim is between the red and yellow flags the lifesavers put up when they're on patrol. Not only is the water safest, but that's the area where they're watching closely to make sure no one gets into trouble.

'So you don't have to worry, Rachel,' Damo said. 'You can just have fun.'

He dived under a wave and surfaced on the other side, with his big wide smile to emphasise his point.

While we were watching, Grampa Jack's patrol had to do a rescue: the first one of the season.

This young woman had dived into a patch of water where the waves weren't breaking, thinking it was safe, but she didn't know the waves weren't breaking there because there was a rip. All was well one moment, the next there was a lot of shouting and just as quickly the beltman was pulling the belt over his head as he was running towards the water. The reelmen secured the reel while the other members of the squad payed out the rescue line, running it out over their heads so that it wouldn't get tangled on anything and so it went further out into the surf before it became submerged and started to drag. A crowd started to gather, drawn by the commotion, but the lifesavers weren't distracted. Everyone did his job with the reel as the beltman swam out to the woman in trouble, diving under waves as he went.

When the beltman reached the woman, who was out behind the break, he grabbed her from behind, left arm around her body with his hand under her chin to support her head, then he started swimming with his free right arm and scissor kicking with his legs (which we couldn't see because they were under water but we all knew that was what he was doing) while the reelmen started winding him back to the beach. They were careful, when waves came, not to wind too hard in case they broke the line, and it was only a minute before the woman was safely on the shore. There she was lifted and carried up the beach and then lowered to the sand beyond the waves. The woman was just tired, and took a little while to recover. Then she was fine. A couple of lifesavers stayed with her to make sure she was all right while others kept watch on the other swimmers and the rest of the squad got the reel ready for the next rescue. There might not be another for the day, or there might be ten or twenty, but they always had to be ready. That's the Bondi lifesavers' motto, although the way they say it sounds funny: *Ready, aye ready.*

People were patting the lifesavers on the back, grateful for what they did. Then everyone went back to enjoying the day. It's strange that way. There could have been a tragedy, but the lifesavers were there, and so nothing bad happened. I reckon the beach is the only place where you can see someone actually save someone's life, and it's treated like it's nothing out of the ordinary. It's just an everyday occurrence. But that doesn't change the fact that you can sit on your towel and watch these big tanned lifesavers diving into the surf and being real-life heroes. I so hope I'll be good enough to be one of them.

Not everyone went swimming today. A lot of people walked down to the water's edge and decided the water was too cold or just took a quick plunge. It didn't matter. They were at Bondi and that's what's important. All the things that are part of summer at Bondi started today: there was the McDonald's surf-o-plane hire and their beach chair hire. The Icebergs were still swimming, but they weren't really Icebergs now that winter was over. Of course, when we went to go to the pictures, we couldn't get a seat on the tram, even though it was a double. That's also part of Bondi in summer. Standing room only.

Sunday, 5 September 1937

Another sign that summer is here is the Sunday night promenade. Tonight was the first time the Bondi Beach Band played on the stand behind the Pavilion. Mum and Dad and Josie and me got dressed, not in our best clothes, but still neat and tidy, and then we went down and joined all the other people, thousands and thousands of them, who were walking up and down the concourse that runs along the back of the beach. There are lights all the way along so people can come and walk up and down long after it gets dark. A few people hire chairs so they can sit and listen to the band, but most people just walk along, every now and then stopping to chat to people that they know.

Us kids are expected to be on our best behaviour, me and Josie walking along with Mum and Dad. Not that they do much walking. If it's not some businessman who doesn't know Dad and wants to talk to him, then it's someone local that Mum has known for years. We get introduced and I have to give each man a firm handshake and say, 'Pleased to meet you'. For some reason I'm not allowed to say, 'Pleased to meet ya'. Josie just has to curtsey, which she really likes doing anyway.

Of course some of the people we meet we know very well, like Rachel and her parents and Damo and his parents. We could have all walked down for the promenade together, but that's not the idea. You go separately and then you meet, accidentally like, and say how pleased you are to see each other. It's a bit of a grownup game, but it's fun to play.

'Pleased to meet you, Rachel.'

'Pleased to meet you, David.'

'Pleased to meet you, Damo.'

'Pleased to meet you, Nipper.'

'Is just like Germany,' Rachel said, after we'd shaken hands. 'Very formal and polite.'

That is, until it started getting late and all us kids started getting impatient because we knew what was coming next: fish and chips or milkshakes up at Powell's, or Milly the Fly or the Greeks'. You beauty! What a perfect way to start the summer. The only thing missing was there was no shark fishing. Mustn't have been any sharks about. I'll have to explain about that sometime.

Oh yes, and the waves today were beaut. The breakers weren't too big but there was a good bank to stand on to catch them. We managed to get Rachel to come out into deeper water to catch a wave but she wasn't very good. She was still a bit nervous even though she was perfectly safe between the flags. Plus she was surrounded by us Bondi kids. We could make sure she was all right too.

Especially me. I still haven't mentioned to anyone that I've been coming down and practising swimming out through the breakers and back again. Now that everyone is swimming nearly every day, they don't even notice when I'm doing it. I just think 'go' and turn and dive and head straight out through the waves. I head all the way out behind the surf then turn back. Body surf a bit, and then go again. Sometimes if I see a lifesaver swimming out, even if it's just for a swim, I go out as well, to see if I can keep up.

Monday, 6 September 1937

Hey diary. I don't think I mentioned that what is even better is that today is the start of the spring school holidays. Normally they're a week after 'summer' starts but this year summer was a bit later. So now it's beach every day and no Mrs Kearsley for two weeks. We went down for most of the day. Then we went exploring around the rocks. We found the rock ledge that this old lady called Bondi Mary, who scavenges around the beach, uses for shelter. There was a dirty old blanket, some old rags and piles of old newspapers, but the old lady wasn't there. She was off foraging somewhere.

Bondi Mary's been wandering around for as long as I can remember, dressed in rags, with an old army overcoat and worn-out sandshoes. She picks through the garbage bins looking for scraps, mumbling to herself. She never speaks to anyone, and she doesn't answer if anyone talks to her. Apart from the way she smells and the strange wild sight of her, she doesn't bother anyone. When us kids have tried to tease her, she's just ignored us. We got bored with trying long ago and left her to her rummaging. Now if someone tries to tease her, most likely a local will tell them to leave her alone.

Sometimes we don't see Bondi Mary for weeks and start wondering where she's gone. Other times she's about on the beach nearly every day, especially on the weekends, when there are more food scraps in the bins. Sometimes the police come and take her away, clean her up and give her some better clothes to wear. Eventually she comes back, dressed in rags rather than the clothes they gave her. She keeps coming back to Bondi.

When Grampa Jack and I go fishing early in the morning, we sometimes see her sleeping under the two piers that run from the Bondi Pavilion down to the water. Sometimes we see her rummaging about on the rocks, right on dawn. She'd be out and about.

She's quite tall and always wears her greatcoat. Never takes it off. Even in summer. Often she wears an old hat, a straw hat or something that looks like she made it from the different scraps she finds.

Wednesday, 8 September 1937

Today Damo, Josie and I took Rachel up exploring behind the houses on North Bondi. There are rocky outcrops and great views of the sea, and if you're lucky, you can sometimes see a whale spouting. Not very often though, because they've been mostly hunted out by whaling stations up and down the coast.

Rachel was really interested in the rock carvings that are over on the other side of the disappearing gun, which was used in olden times to protect Sydney. There was one carving of a whale that she particularly liked, and carvings of people and fish and even footprints.

'Aboriginal people carved them,' I told her.

'Where are the Aboriginal people now?' she asked.

'They're still around. They've got humpies in among the rocks, out along the headland there. You sometimes see 'em fishin' around the harbour or off the rocks on the headland. Not so much these days, but sometimes.'

'Do they have their own language?' Rachel asked.

'I think so,' I answered. 'I know *Bondi* is Aboriginal. It means breaking water, or surf, or something.'

'Maybe they will come and drive us away, if Bondi is their place,' Rachel said.

'I don't think so,' I said. 'They pretty much keep to themselves. Not friendly, you know. Now see there, that's a footprint.'

'What do they wear?'

'The ones I've seen, mostly dirty old clothes. I think charities give them stuff so they won't be naked. They used to have no clothes at all, from what we learned at school.'

I don't know why but Rachel was really keen to see one of these Aboriginal people for real. So we told her we'd take her out along South Head sometime. It's mostly just farms and rock quarries and scrub out there, but there are still some of the old people about.

The beach was perfect again today. Sunny, almost no wind, and waves not too big and not too small. Grampa Jack is on patrol as a beach inspector most days now and will be all through summer. In winter he usually does odd jobs for the council, where he works. The funny thing is, most of the beach inspectors, who are employed by the council, are also part of the volunteer lifesaving clubs. So when they're not getting paid to save people's lives, they're doing it for free.

The reason there's two organisations is because

the council wanted to make sure the beach always had someone on patrol. So since 1913 (when Dinny Brown became the first beach inspector) some lifesavers have been paid, especially during the week when most volunteer lifesavers have to work, to ensure there's always someone on patrol. No surprise that most beach inspectors come from surf lifesaving. That's my dream job, actually, being a beach inspector like Grampa Jack. That way I could spend all summer saving people at Bondi.

Saturday, 11 September 1937

Hey diary, the weekenders have started settling in. In case you don't know, there's about four or five houses that lifesavers from places like Paddington, Waverley and Bondi Junction rent around our place at North Bondi. Every house has a name. There's *Arcadia, Solstice, Rose Cottage, Doralian* and *Sluggers Camp*. Some houses have someone who maybe doesn't have a job looking after the place during the week and then the rest of the weekenders come out on Friday or early Saturday to go on patrol with the lifesavers. They stay the whole weekend, then go home late Sunday to be ready for work on Monday. They all chip in for the rent, about twenty or thirty shillings a week, out of their own pockets, just so they can spend their weekends being volunteer lifesavers. They pay that for the privilege of doing lifesaving patrols for free.

Grampa Jack, Damo, Rachel and I helped the fellas at the weekender called Rose Cottage move in. They were mates of Grampa Jack's, but us kids had our own reason for helping. Rose Cottage is only small – two bedrooms and a kitchen – but the yard is so big they've made their own mini-golf course. It's just a few holes and various obstacles to hit your ball around, but the lifesavers are always inventing new challenges to make it more interesting. Anyway, because we helped them move in, they let us play mini-golf.

We played around while Grampa Jack sat on a banana box and watched. Then he started telling one of his stories.

'Do you all know about Nosey Bob, the Hangman?' he asked.

I'd heard about him heaps of times. Damo too. But Rachel hadn't, so Grampa Jack was off.

'Nosey used to live up on Ben Buckler, back before

the turn of the century, when it was known as O'Brien's Bush. He was once a good-lookin' fella, they reckon, and he used to drive a hansom cab, a horse-drawn taxi, taking the posh folk from Darling Point to wherever they wanted to go. Then one day, one of his horses gave a kick and caught him in the face. Made a real mess and he was disfigured for life. That's how he became known as Nosey Bob.

'Trouble was, the society ladies couldn't bear to look at him, so his business started to fail. He had to sell out and then he couldn't get another job, on account of being so badly scarred. Eventually, the only job he could get was as the hangman at Darlinghurst Gaol. For thirty years he gave dozens of wrongdoers the drop, but the funny thing was, he always tried to do the right thing by the families of the blokes he sent to their maker. Some of them ended up calling him "the gentleman hangman" instead of "Nosey Bob" but it didn't make much difference. His wife had stuck by him but she ended up dying of a broken heart because people were so horrible to Nosey after his accident, and worse still when he became a hangman.

'Now this Nosey, he was one of the first people to

start shark fishing. Years ago, he'd fish for them off the beach, then when one was caught, he'd wade in and tail it – put a rope around its tail. Then he'd use his horse to pull it out of the water. His house used to be surrounded with the jaws of the sharks he'd caught. The place was just like any other shack, but when we were kids we'd stay well away. We reckoned if the sharks didn't get you, the ghosts of the people he'd hanged would.'

'Is the house still there?' Rachel asked

'Long gone, like old Nosey,' he said. 'It's a block of flats now. Reckon even the ghosts have moved on now.'

After we played mini-golf, we went and played in the sandhills between Bondi and Rose Bay. It was funny the way Blair Street just ended in sand. The dunes were almost completely bare – just a few bits of bush. Grampa Jack reckons there used to be nothing but dunes on the north side of Bondi once, from the beach all the way back. Then they bulldozed the sand away and built houses. They were still pushing the sand away and building things. Every year a little bit more. Lots of people wanted to live at Bondi, or near it, and new houses were going up on the hill on the north side of the beach.

Sunday, 12 September 1937

Not such a nice day today. There was a bit of bad weather in the morning, rainy and squally, and grey choppy waves. It was quite cold but it started clearing in the afternoon, which meant the Sunday evening promenade was on, and the band was playing. Really, it has to be chucking it down raining for people not to promenade.

Rachel got to see the shark fishing. She'd heard Grampa Jack talking about it and wondered if it was true. Tonight, during the Sunday promenade, she got to see it for real. While everyone was walking up and down, there were about half a dozen blokes, all local fellas, down on the beach. They were baiting up, throwing their lines in and getting ready to fish long into the night. I pointed them out to Rachel and we watched for a while until there was a huge commotion, which meant someone had caught a shark.

The fisherman started hauling in on his line until the shark was thrashing around in the surf. By then a crowd had gathered on the shore. A few of the local fellas were pretty brave and they took a rope out into the water.

'They're called *the tailers*,' Grampa Jack explained

to Rachel. 'When they get the rope around the shark's tail, that's when the real fun begins.'

The shark was big. Maybe ten or twelve feet long. Two fellas got to the shark, which was still trying to swim away from the beach. One grabbed the tail and the other wrapped the rope around it. Then all the other fishermen and tailers started hauling on the rope. Must have been about fifteen of them dragging at this shark that's still thrashing in the surf. Slowly they'd dragged it up on to the beach. Huge thing it was, with a cold black eye and jaws still snapping. No one went near the jaws. Grampa Jack said the jaws can still snap even after the shark is dead. It's got a nerve that will trigger a reaction if it's touched.

'You could lose a finger or your hand, or even your whole arm,' I told Rachel.

She actually shuddered at the thought.

'Maybe that's what happened in the Shark Arm Case,' Grampa Jack said, giving me a wink.

Rachel couldn't help but take the bait. 'What is this?' she asked.

'Nipper, you know the story,' Grampa Jack said. Everyone knew the story.

'See, someone caught this big tiger shark,' I explained, 'just off Coogee Beach, still alive, and they put it in the big aquarium down there. It was only there a week when it got sick. Then it had a big spew, you know, *bleuhh*, right there in the aquarium. Some people actually saw it throw up a human arm.'

Rachel put a hand to her mouth. 'That's terrible,' she said.

'That's not all,' Grampa Jack said. 'What happened next, Nipper?'

'They worked out whose arm it was,' I answered. 'The arm had a tattoo of two boxers, shaping for a fight, and that was the same tattoo a local gangster named Jim Smith had.'

'Then they worked out that the shark hadn't bitten Jim Smith's arm off,' Grampa Jack added. 'Someone had cut it off first.'

It was a grisly tale, but like everyone in Sydney at the time, Rachel had to know more. 'Did they ever find out who did it?'

'They know who did it,' I said, 'but he got away with it. This bloke named Brady was one of Smith's partners in crime and he was charged with Smith's murder. Then his lawyer got up and said, "You've only got Smith's arm. Where's his body? For all you know, Smith could still be alive. You've got no case".'

'And Brady got away with it?' Rachel gasped.

'That's right,' Grampa Jack said. 'That was two years ago, and there hasn't been a sign of Jim Smith since.'

Then another shark was caught, a bit further along the beach, and everyone rushed off to tail that one.

Monday, 13 September 1937

This morning there were nearly a dozen dead sharks lying on the beach. It was a bit sad the way those sharks were just left to rot, just so someone could brag about the shark they caught or the one they went into the surf and tailed. After a while, some council workers came down and dug a big pit to dump the sharks in. They dug down about six feet or more so the smell wouldn't come back up. And next Sunday night, if there were sharks about, the fishermen would be back, putting on a show. And on Monday someone would have to bury them. It was like that all through summer, until there were dozens of holes with all these dead sharks in them.

Most nights the shark fishermen wouldn't even keep the jaws. There were so many shark jaws hanging up around Bondi, no one could be bothered with them.

The council didn't seem to mind the shark fishing even though it meant they had to clean up all the sharks the next day. Maybe they thought it kept the numbers down, and it made an interesting spectacle for all the visitors who came down to Bondi on a Sunday.

Sometimes one of the beach inspectors, Aub Laidlaw, would help the shark fishermen. He had a mate who'd ask him to take his bait out, right on sunset. Aub would grab the bait and line, hook them on to his swimming trunks and swim out through the breakers. He'd go right out to the channel behind the breakers, where the sharks were, and dump the bait. Then he'd catch a couple of waves back to the beach. Sometimes his mate would have hooked a shark before Aub was even back on the shore.

'That Aub,' Grampa Jack said as he watched him. 'He isn't afraid of anything, let alone sharks.'

Grampa Jack wasn't scared of sharks either. When the weather was good and he took me out in his little dinghy, fishing on the sea, we'd be there in a twelve-foot boat with fourteen-foot sharks swimming past. All Grampa Jack would say when I caught a fish was 'Reel 'im in quick, Nipper, or all you'll get is the head. Them noahs'll take the rest.'

He calls sharks *noahs* because Noah's Ark rhymes with shark.

'Did I ever tell you 'bout the time I swam over a noah?' he told me once when we were out fishing.

'Lots of times,' I said, but it didn't make any difference. He told me anyway.

'I was in a swimming race. Me and another Bondi lifesaver were representing Bondi. We were in the lead, swam out to the rounding buoy and didn't hear the bell they used to ring to warn of a shark. All the other swimmers were standing on the beach. Me and this other fella were the only ones out there. We rounded the buoy, started heading in, and I was wondering where everyone was. Then I'm looking down, and there's this shape down in the water. The noah. But he weren't a very big one. So we just kept goin'. Well, the best thing was to keep headin' for the beach.

'That's where we found out there were two noahs, and the other one was much bigger.'

Tuesday, 14 September 1937

Today Mum, Josie and I went on the train to Singleton to visit Jamie at Uncle Neville and Auntie May's farm. The train ride was beaut. There was a big green steam engine, numbered 3635, huffing steam and blowing soot, then whistling and chuffing out of Central Station. The best part of the trip was when we crossed the Hawkesbury River on a big steel bridge that went right across this huge, wide stretch of water. On the other side we went through a big tunnel and came out beside this creek. The train ran all along the water for ages before it went into another big tunnel. There were all these places growing oysters and there were houses you could only reach by boat. What a great life that would be.

Jamie and Uncle Neville met us at the station at Singleton. Jamie has grown really tall. He's almost as big as Mum. And he's really strong – from all the farm work he's doing, he reckons. He tossed our bags on to Uncle Neville's truck, and Mum and Josie got in the front while Jamie and I sat on the back.

Jamie knew everything about the places along the way to the farm, and was waving to lots of people he saw as well. It took a while too, because Uncle Neville had to stop for a chin-wag with some of the people on the road.

Auntie May was nice as ever. She had hot scones and jam and cream ready when we arrived, for afternoon tea. We chucked my bag into the sleepout where Jamie sleeps and then came back and 'cleaned up them scones' as Uncle Neville put it. Plus there was lemonade, but not fizzy like it is in Bondi – this was made from real lemons from Auntie May's trees.

Then the cows started walking up to the milking shed. They knew it was time to be milked and they came up without anyone having to go and get them. There were about sixty cows, and there was no way we could have milked them all, except the milking shed has a milking machine. Jamie showed me how to put the cows into the stalls, where they ate some hay and he put these tubes on their udders. I was a bit scared by the cows, because they were really big, but they turned out to be very gentle. Even so, Jamie said to be careful.

'They might not mean to hurt you but if they bump you or tread on you, you'll know it. And never get between the greedy ones and some hay,' he said. 'Or stand behind them in case they kick, or poo all over you.'

Jamie knows everything about cows. Well, he knows everything about everything.

After the cows were milked we took the milk cans to the front gate and loaded them on to a truck that gathers all the milk from the farms in the area. Then it goes to Singleton to meet the milk train that goes to Sydney every day. Uncle Neville reckons we probably drink the milk from his farm when we have a milkshake in Bondi.

Back at the house Auntie May and Mum had a great meal ready for us. Corned beef and boiled potatoes, peas and carrots and white sauce (on the side, so if you didn't like it, you didn't have to have it) and then ice cream and jelly for desert. And all the milk you could drink.

Not long after dinner we went to bed. It was only just after eight o'clock but it had been a long day and Mum, Josie and I were really sleepy. And it seems that on a farm that's when everyone goes to bed anyway. Jamie said goodnight and fell straight to sleep but he let me have the light on so I could write my diary.

Wednesday, 15 September 1937

I'm so tired. Jamie woke me at five o'clock this morning

to go and milk the cows. I could hardly stay awake, and it was still completely dark when we started putting the cows into the stalls.

'You get used to it,' Jamie said, while I kept nodding off in between filling up the hay bales.

He was full of energy while he hosed out the milking shed and then loaded the milk cans on to Uncle Neville's little truck. After that we ate a huge breakfast of eggs and toast and all the milk we could drink. Meanwhile, Mum and Josie were sleeping! Talk about lucky. We had to wake Mum and Josie so they could have breakfast, when we'd been up for hours.

As soon as we finished breakfast we went out and started taking big bales of hay to the cows, then we got the tractor and scraped some special piece of equipment up and down a paddock that did something to the ground that had something to do with getting more hay. After lunch Uncle Neville gave Jamie some time off to show us around. We had a look at his horse, Mrs K, and he saddled her up and gave us rides. He led Josie around, then let her ride around the yard on her own. She seemed to really like it. I had a turn too, but I was scared I'd fall off. Then Jamie got on and showed us how he could make her trot and canter and turn quickly, like she was mustering stray cattle.

We went for a walk along the small river that winds past the farm. It's called the Wollombi Brook, and Jamie reckons there's heaps of fish and yabbies that he catches on his day off, when he's not riding with some of the boys and girls from the nearby farms.

After that, more milking, then dinner and finally, bed. I'd be asleep already but I'm so tired, I'm not sure I'll remember everything and be able to write it down tomorrow.

Thursday, 16 September 1937

Even more tired. I didn't think it was possible but it is. Today's routine was much the same as yesterday, except we did some fencing, and tried to fix a broken pump, and carried water in buckets to the trough the pump was supposed to fill. I was sitting by the road with Uncle Neville waiting for the milk truck when I asked him if Dad used to do all these farm chores when he lived on the farm.

'Yeah,' Uncle Neville said, 'but he hated it.'

'Really?' I said. I was beginning to understand why.

'Yeah,' Uncle Neville said. 'There's some just ain't suited to it.'

'Jamie seems to like it,' I said.

'Yeah. Good for anything, that one.'

Jamie was putting the cows into a new paddock with another bale of hay.

'Your dad, though,' Uncle Neville said, 'he was meant for other things. I still don't know exactly what he does at the bank, but we'd be stuffed without him.'

'Why's that?' I asked. I was glad there was a grownup who didn't have a clue what Dad did either.

'He's got a great head for numbers, your dad. And for business. It was him worked out how we could keep the farm goin' with milking machines. And make it pay.'

'Maybe he just hated milking cows,' I joked. Uncle Neville laughed too.

'I don't doubt that,' he said. 'But he was a lifesaver for me and Auntie May. We couldn't have kept the place goin' on our own. He's a good man, your dad. Real good. And there's a lot of people down Bondi way reckon so too.'

'Why's that?'

'In the dark times, few years back, the banks woulda

sold 'em up. All them little businesses. But your dad stood up for 'em. Saved quite a few.'

I'd never thought of dad as a lifesaver. Well, considering how badly he swims, who would? But I guess there's more than one way to save people.

Friday, 17 September 1937

Three days of getting up at five o'clock and I'm thinking I must be like Dad. Every day I'm more tired than the day before. I don't know how Jamie does it, or why he loves it so much.

It was real sad saying goodbye at the train station. Everyone started crying, even Jamie, because it'll be Christmas before we see him again. I slept most of the way back to Sydney on the train.

The beach looked strange when we got back there in the late afternoon. Even Josie noticed it.

'Mum, the beach looks funny,' she said.

'Of course it does,' Mum said. 'When you see it every day, it always looks familiar. When you see it for the first time after you've been away, it's never quite the same.'

Still, it was good to be home. And some things

hadn't changed. I met up with Grampa Jack and told him all about the farm, and how hard it was getting up to milk the cows.

'You don't seem to mind gettin' up to go fishin', he said.

'Not every day, Grampa,' I said. 'Those cows don't even take weekends off.'

Now, would you believe, I can't sleep. I put my diary away and went to bed, but I'm still wide awake. I keep thinking about leaving school next year and going to work with Jamie up on the farm. Now I'm not sure if I could do it. And Mum and Dad aren't keen for me to be a delivery boy for Mr Smith until I'm old enough to be a lifesaver, and then a beach inspector. In the meantime, Mrs Kearsley keeps saying I'll end up like my brother. Well, what if I can't even do that? If only I was older and could be a lifesaver. Everything would be simpler then.

Saturday, 18 September 1937

Today was one of the most important days for anyone who wants to be a Bondi lifesaver. Down at the beach, all the local kids who have turned sixteen, and some older blokes who were hoping to get involved in lifesaving, were trying to get their bronze medallions. You have to qualify for that to become a lifesaver, plus be sixteen, and a boy, because girls aren't allowed. They couldn't even do the bronze medallion. For that you needed to prove you were a good swimmer, and swim four hundred yards in under thirteen minutes, then swim fifty yards, pick up a person who needed rescuing and tow them fifty yards. You also had to know what to do if someone wasn't breathing, which meant how to use the Schafer method, the technique lifesavers used to revive someone who has drowned.

Just about every kid in Bondi from about ten years old could get their bronze medallion if they were allowed, but sometimes you'd see the weekenders, people from other areas who wanted to be lifesavers, struggle to do the swim. Some would get really upset if they didn't make it. And then, even if you got your bronze medallion, you weren't guaranteed to be let into a lifesaving club. If a member had a good reason why you couldn't be trusted, they could refuse to take you. Or if you brought shame on your club or misbehaved they'd send you on your way. And then you had to have the money to pay the membership. Lifesavers weren't just unpaid for the time they spent saving lives – they had to pay membership fees for the privilege.

You'd think that would discourage most people, but it was the opposite. If you were a lifesaver, even if you hadn't saved anyone, nearly everybody looked up to you. And every day you were standing alongside blokes who really were heroes, like Aub Laidlaw and Grampa Jack and lots of other blokes. Everyone thought those blokes were the best, especially us kids. If we were mucking around and they told us to stop, we did. We all wanted to be them one day, and we didn't want any of them to decide we couldn't because we wouldn't do as we were told.

Of course, once you were in the lifesavers, that was just the beginning. You had to learn how to do rescues, how to work on the reel or swim with the belt, how to march and how to row in the surf boat and lots of other stuff. When they weren't on patrol, lifesavers were practising and doing drills and learning more about the surf. The older blokes taught them everything they needed to know.

After watching people go for their bronze medallion, I went into the surf and tried to see if I could qualify. I dived out through the breakers, and then out the back I tried to swim along for what I reckoned was four hundred yards. That's nearly halfway down the beach. So I started swimming and next thing I know, there's a lifesaver swimming out to me with a belt.

'Oh, it's you, Nipper,' he said when he got to me. 'What are you doin' swimmin' outside the flags?'

I couldn't tell him the real reason, so like an idiot I said, 'Oh, sorry. I forgot.'

'You forgot!' He obviously didn't believe me. 'Maybe you should come back to the beach until you remember.'

Thank goodness he let me swim in on my own. It would have been really embarrassing to get rescued. I'd never hear the end of it.

Sunday, 19 September 1937

'There is rip.' Rachel pointed.

'That's right,' Grampa Jack said. At the Sunday promenade, us kids were showing off how much we'd taught Rachel about the surf.

'There is rip.' Rachel pointed again.

'Well spotted, Rachel,' Grampa Jack said.

Then she looked towards North Bondi. We could all see a small rip, hiding under the rising tide and some sloppy waves, but it was there. I think Grampa Jack, Damo and I were holding our breath.

'Might be rip.' She pointed. 'But I don't swim anyway. Waves are rubbish for surf-o-plane.'

We all laughed. That was good enough.

'You might have taught her too well,' Grampa Jack muttered.

Monday, 20 September 1937

Back to school today. Old Mrs Kearsley again. But only one more term and I'll be done with her. I can't wait.

Today was a sad day for Grampa Jack. It's the anniversary of the day Grandma Doris died. It was a long time ago but Grampa Jack always takes flowers to put on her grave. I was too young to know Grandma Doris, but Mum says she was really nice. She was a country girl, like Dad was a country boy, who came down to Sydney to work. Grandma Doris and Grampa Jack started out living in a little one-bedroom unit just back from the middle of Bondi for a few years then got a little cottage up the northern end. Grandma Doris loved the surf but she got skin cancer and died when Mum was a teenager. Grampa Jack has been living in their house ever since. He sometimes says we should move in with him but Mum likes it where she is, looking out over Bondi.

Because of what happened to Grandma Doris, Mum is always going on about not getting too much sun. She always has this great big bag that she takes down to the beach. It's full of zinc cream, to stop sunburn, plus every other thing in case you need it at the beach – sandwiches, soft drink, napkins, plastic cups, sting cream, vinegar (for bluebottle stings), boiled lollies (to take the salty taste out of your mouth) and lots of other stuff. Most kids in Bondi know that if they have anything from sunburn to tummy ache, Mum will have something in her bag to help.

Grampa Jack reckons Grandma Doris might have been from the country, but she was still a beach girl.

'All the lifesavers fall for beach girls,' he says. 'The girls that are always at the beach. And all the beach girls fall for lifesavers.'

He might have been right, but it wasn't so with Mum and Dad. Mum was a beach girl but Dad was a country boy. Well, he came from the country, though he's not a country person like Uncle Neville. Anyway, Grampa reckons Mum never worried about too much sun until Grandma died.

Just like Grampa and Grandma, once Mum and Dad married, they tried to find a place to live at Bondi. That was their idea of heaven. Married, living by the sea. I suppose that's what will happen to me. I'll become a lifesaver, marry a beach girl and go to the beach. I'd do it every day of my life if I could. Maybe I could marry Rachel, although I think she likes Damo more than me.

I'm starting to understand, though, why it is people from other areas want to come to Bondi and become lifesavers. When you become a lifesaver, it's like you've got a second family. The other lifesavers are like your brothers, and the rest of Bondi is your family. Who wouldn't want to be part of that? So I reckon maybe I won't go and work on the farm. I'd rather stay here. Except I don't know what I'll do until I'm sixteen.

Thursday, 23 September 1937

Gee, four hundred yards is a long way. It's even further

after a wave breaks on you and you breathe in some water. I was out there early this morning, before the beach inspectors were on duty so they couldn't tell me to swim between the flags, trying to qualify for the bronze medallion.

I was treading water while I coughed and gasped, and this bloke swims up, doing laps of the whole beach, and he goes, 'You all right, kid?'

He thought I needed rescuing. Actually, I nearly did.

'Yeah,' I croaked. 'I'm right.'

'If you want to ocean swim,' he said, 'you've got to focus on two things: the ocean part and the swimming part.'

Well, obviously. Anyway, I felt too crook to keep going. So I headed in. Reckon I'd got about two hundred yards.

Saturday, 25 September 1937

Hey diary. Remember how, a while back, Damo and I told Rachel we'd show her the Aboriginal people who live around South Head? Well, today we met this nice old bloke. We were supposed to be going to the pictures but

Rachel suggested we go and explore around on South Head. So we walked to Rose Bay, took the bus out to Vaucluse, on Sydney Harbour, then went walking out past Camp Cove. There's a naval base there, but you can still walk along the shore, and that's where we came upon this tin humpy, tucked into the bush a bit. It was just like the other shacks you see around the place, where people have been living since the big Depression, a few years ago.

It was bad times during the Depression. Lots of people didn't have jobs and had to get food handouts just to live. Many of them ended up homeless, which was why they built shelters out of anything they could find. Or they lived in caves. The Depression started around 1929, when I really was just a nipper, and was at its worst in 1932. Things are supposed to have improved, but there are still hawkers going from house to house all the time. And when kids come to school without any shoes, no one says anything. Damo was one of those kids for a long, long time. His dad went for years without a job. They had to get by on whatever work he could get from day to day, queuing at factories or building sites for anything that was going.

Anyway, there was an old bloke sitting outside this

old humpy house. Damo and I were too scared to go any closer. We were afraid he might yell at us or something, so we kind of hung on the edge of the scrub. I reckon this bloke must have known we were there but he didn't do anything.

So Rachel says, 'You coming?' and when she saw we weren't, she just left us and walked straight up to him.

'Hello, my name's Rachel,' she said.

The old fella looked her up and down and said, 'Hello, Rachel. Me name's Arthur.'

Rachel then turned and pointed at us, still standing a bit of a ways off, and told Arthur our names, 'Damo and David'.

And Arthur called out, 'They call ya Nipper, don't they?'

It turned out he knew Grampa Jack. He also knew that I was Grampa Jack's grandson. I don't know how he knew, but he did. Anyway, Arthur turned out not to mind us having a bit of a yarn with him. He'd lived around South Head all his life but he thought he'd have to move away soon.

'Gettin' too crowded,' he said.

He said he liked catching things to eat and finding

tucker in the bush, but that was getting scarce because people kept turning the bush into houses.

'There's not much room left for us blackfellas,' he said. 'Every year, bit of country gets gobbled up, so people move away.'

'Where do they go?' Rachel asked.

'Lapa,' Arthur said.

'Where?' I'd never heard of it.

'La Perouse,' Arthur said. 'Down Botany Bay. You know, where all the trouble started.'

'What trouble's that?' Damo asked.

'Whitefella trouble,' Arthur said. 'That's where Cap'n Cook come and then they started takin' everythin'. Don't they teach you history no more?'

'Oh, that trouble,' we chorused. He was talking about a hundred and fifty years ago.

'Funny thing though,' Arthur said, 'that Lapa, it's still our country. They taken nearly everything else but they never took that.'

We talked like that for a bit, then Arthur hunted us off.

'Can't sit yarnin' all day,' he said. But then he said to me and Damo, 'It's good to finally meet you fellas.'

It was like he knew us. I don't know why we didn't know him.

Monday, 27 September 1937

Turns out Grampa Jack had known Arthur for years.

'He gets around a fair bit,' Grampa Jack said. 'Keeps to himself mostly though.'

'He reckons he knows me,' I said. 'He knew my nickname.'

'Yeah,' Grampa said. 'He doesn't miss much. I might've mentioned you back in those tough years, the Depression and that. Back then, when I'd go fishing over at the harbour, see if I could get a feed, I'd see Arthur and we'd share our fish if one of us had some luck. Still see him now and then, just to say g'day. But not so much any more. Must be getting too old or something.'

Tuesday, 19 October 1937

Mrs Kearsley is at me again. Today she started talking about the Primary Final exam, which is held at the beginning of next month. You take the test to see if you can go on with your education, like to high school, and if you can get some money from the government to do it. Mrs Kearsley told us what we could do to prepare for the exam but that some of us didn't need to bother.

'Mr McCutcheon, for example, will probably be finishing his education, such as it is, this year. So he won't need to sit the Primary Final.'

I thought that would be great, although if I finish school I dunno what I'll end up doing. Tonight, at dinner, I mentioned it to Mum and Dad.

'Of course you'll do the final,' Dad said. 'And go to Sydney High, and after that, you're smart enough to go to university.'

'But that means years and years of school.' I was horrified at the thought. And Sydney High? You had to be really clever to go there. Even if I was, I'd be the only one from my school who'd go. I wouldn't know anyone.

And there's really only one test I want to pass. The bronze medallion – four hundred yards, fifty yards before you save someone, then fifty yards saving them. I reckon I can already do the fifties. The four hundred I'm working on. It's tougher than you'd think, especially if you do it in the sea. I'm still trying to get there. I reckon if I can swim from the rocks at North Bondi down to the Pavilion in the middle of the beach, it'll count. There's a trick to it, but. You really do have to watch out for the waves and change the way you swim to deal with them.

Wednesday, 20 October 1937

Rachel reckons I should do the Primary Final.

'You're the smartest kid in school,' she said, which was nice to be told. 'Don't listen to Mrs Kearsley. Now's your chance to prove her wrong.'

'I'm not the smartest kid in school – you are,' I said, although I wouldn't mind making Mrs Kearsley eat humble pie.

'Are you afraid a girl might beat you?' she said, and gave me a shove. So I shoved her back. Then I chased her all the way home.

Later, looking at the waves with Grampa Jack (a clean smooth break, good for body surfing but a little on the small side), he started asking me questions, like 'What's eight times seven?'

'Fifty-six.'

'Six times five.'

'That's kid's stuff. Thirty.'

'How much of *The Man from Snowy River* do you know?'

'All of it.'

'Why don't you think you can do the Primary Final?'

That was a toughie.

Thursday, 21 October 1937

I'm doing the exam. We're all doing the exam. I knew Rachel would do it but when I asked Damo, he just said, 'Yeah, of course.'

'How come of course?'

'I want to be a fireman,' he said. 'You can't get in if you leave school at thirteen.'

'You can be a lifesaver,' I said.

Damo just looked at me and said, 'Is that all you want to be?'

I didn't answer him but I thought, yeah, that's all I want to be. Isn't that enough?

Saturday, 23 October 1937

Great day at the beach today. A man gave me two empty soft-drink bottles that he didn't want to take back to the shop, so Rachel, Damo and I hired a surf-o-plane for a whole half hour. It was beaut.

I should probably explain what a surf-o-plane is, although the best way to find out is to go to the beach and try one. They're inflatable rubber mats that make it really easy for just about anyone to surf a wave. They also help you float, so if you get into deep water and aren't a strong swimmer, all you have to do is hang on to your surf-o-plane and you'll be right.

The surf-o-planes were invented by a real doctor, just a couple of beaches down from Bondi. His name was Dr Ernest Smithers, and they say he spent eight years working on his design. He even got help from his friend, the famous aviator Sir Charles Kingsford Smith, who was also one of the first people ever to be rescued by the lifesavers at Bondi, though not by Grampa Jack.

Dr Smithers wasn't a strong swimmer, so he got another friend, Dr Ping, the local doctor from Bondi, to help him test his invention. Dr Ping is really nice and like everyone from Bondi, he's part fish. He's also famous because he named the horse Phar Lap. Dr Ping is originally Malayan-Chinese, although he comes from Queensland, and Phar Lap is Malayan for lightning.

Anyway, once Dr Smithers perfected his surf-o-plane, they were so good that the Chief Beach Inspector at Bondi, Stan McDonald, quit his job a few years ago so he could run a business hiring them out on the beach. He also hires out deckchairs.

They reckon the first surf-o-plane models were made from old car inner tubes welded together. Now they're made from really tough rubber, usually three or four tubes, and they come in three sizes: small, medium and large. The proper surf-o-planes are yellow and black but there are other brands in different colours, or just black.

You can buy a surf-o-plane but you have to be pretty rich to afford one. Most people hire them from Mr McDonald instead, assuming they've got the money. That's why you'll see a lot of us kids scavenging bottles and searching the shore for lost coins, to get enough money to hire a surf-o-plane. Then it's out into the waves to have a surf. It's a lot easier than trying to ride a surfboard, and heaps cheaper. The lifesaving clubs have a few surfboards but only some of the lifesavers are good enough to use them.

Tuesday, 26 October 1937

Even Mr Smith reckons I should do the Primary Final. I mentioned to him my idea about maybe going to work for him doing deliveries if I quit school. He said it was no go.

'It's not that you wouldn't do a good job,' he said. 'But there's not much of a future in it. You'll get bored and then what? You don't want to end up like all these other blokes moochin' from job to job, no qualifications, taking whatever work they can get. And the worst days of the Depression might be past but look around. There's lots of young blokes who will still work for next to nothing. You might get a job as a beach inspector, but what if you don't?'

Oh, and I saw that Aboriginal fella, Arthur, today. He was down near the beach fossicking in the rock pools when Grampa Jack and I were walking home. I thought he saw us and I waved to him, but he didn't wave back.

'He has funny ways,' Grampa Jack said. 'If he doesn't want to say g'day, leave him be.'

Thursday, 28 October 1937

Lots of controversy around Bondi today. The council has started putting up nets to try to stop sharks coming into the shore. They'll put them out a couple of times a week and they reckon that'll be enough to keep the shark numbers down. And they're gonna put another one up at Coogee, because they have a surf carnival at night there, and they think a net will make it safer.

There was a little trawler came and put the net down but after it was gone, you could hardly tell if the net was there. There were just a couple of floats that gave you a bit of an idea of where it was. The actual net was under the water, down about fifteen feet, so swimmers and boats won't get tangled in it. It goes all the way to the bottom, which Grampa Jack reckons is where the sharks prefer to be, unless they're basking in the sun.

Not everyone is happy about the nets, even though they won't be there all the time. They say a net put up at Newcastle caught a hundred and two sharks in one night. The shark fishermen reckon that'll put an end to their fun.

Wednesday, 3 November 1937

Today was the day of the Primary Final. There were questions about maths, English, history and geography – all the main things we've learned about at school. Most of the questions were easy but you also had to write a short composition describing someone you know. I thought about all the people I could write about, like Grampa Jack or Bondi Mary or even Nosey Bob, the Hangman. Then I decided to write about Arthur.

It was easy to write about him because I've written about him before in my diary. I wrote about how, when we first met, he seemed to know me already but I didn't know him. I said that I'd seen Aboriginal people around Bondi lots of times but I'd never really paid them any attention until I met Arthur and found out they were people just like anyone else. I was going to put something about how Arthur having to leave his home was a bit like Rachel having to leave hers but I ran out of space. Still I thought it was a good story. So now we have to wait a month or so to find out how we did.

Mrs Kearsley is probably hoping I fail, but I'll show her.

Saturday, 6 November 1937

Four hundred! I finally did it. I was too tired to rescue anyone when I got to the beach, but I was right in front of the Pavilion when I got out of the water.

I was burstin' to tell someone but when I got home and I saw Dad was up and about, I just said, 'Hi Dad.'

'Morning, Nip. Want some toast?'

I ate four slices. Dad didn't say anything. He just kept toasting bread and feeding it to me.

Sunday, 7 November 1937

Hey diary. It's been a week since they started putting the shark net down but they reckon they've hardly caught any sharks. Maybe they should have asked the local fishos. They say there's none around at the moment. You've got to get the right tides and moon and stuff for the sharks to come in, after the fish. The council still thinks the shark net will make sure no one gets attacked, but no one's been bitten since 1928 anyway. Either way, the shark fishermen aren't that happy about it. They still fish on a Sunday night, but even they aren't catching much.

I dunno about the net. I mean, there haven't been

that many shark attacks around Bondi, but when they've happened, they're hard to forget. For example, everyone remembers two local lifesavers, Jack Chalmers and Frank Beaurepaire, who rescued a young swimmer, Harry Coughlan, who was attacked by a shark at Coogee back in 1922. Jack was on lifesaving duty and tied a rope around his waist and ran over the rocks to get out to Harry. He fell and nearly knocked himself out but kept going and dived in. There were sharks all around Harry but Jack and then Frank did everything they could to help him. They got him ashore but he died in hospital not long after. Both Jack and Frank got Royal Humane Society gold medals and a cash reward. Jack used his to buy a house. Frank used his to start a business selling tyres. It's pretty successful, and I reckon a lot of the success of Beaurepaire's is because everyone knows the story of how it came about.

Then, when I was just a little tacker, in 1928, there was a shark attack at Bondi. Max Steele was swimming with his brother Harry in the middle of the beach but couldn't catch a wave. Harry gave up but Max stayed out there on his own. The shark got him on the leg. He lost most of it from the knee down. They helped him up to North Bondi Surf Club, but it was locked up. So they broke the locks off to get into the first aid room. The ambulance took him to hospital and he needed blood, so a North Bondi lifesaver rolled up his sleeve and gave the blood he needed. That's why the old fellas in the club reckon they saved Max twice. They didn't save the leg, though. The noah got that.

Maybe it was the same shark that attacked Nita Derrett, also in the 1920s, over at Bronte, except she lost both legs. It was late in the afternoon and she was just paddling in the surf. Now Bronte usually has deep water right near the shore, then a bank, which means the sharks can come right in to the beach. So even if you're only paddling in the water, they can grab your legs. That's what happened to Nita. Funny thing, though, it didn't make her scared to go in the water. You can still see her some days down at the beach going for a swim. She comes down, friends or lifesavers help her to the water, and she goes in and swims.

So that's three shark attacks in fifteen or so years on three beaches. It's not a lot really, even though sharks are about all the time.

Oh, and this morning, another four hundred-yard

swim. It was still hard but I managed it. Towards the end I was getting tired, but I made myself keep going. Got there, exhausted, but pretty pleased with myself.

Tuesday, 9 November 1937

Hey diary, caught a beaut snapper with Grampa Jack today. On school days he usually goes out fishing with a mate in his dinghy, but when his mate can't make it, he sometimes takes me. Four or five in the morning, he comes tappin' on me window.

'Nipper, hey, Nipper,' he goes, in a whispery kind of voice, so he won't wake Mum and Dad. 'Young Nipper, wakey, wakey. They're bitin'.'

'Comin', Grampa Jack,' I whisper back.

He always knows when the conditions are good for launching off this little rock shelf he knows under Ben Buckler. Too much swell, or the tide not right, and you'll get swamped. Or you'll get out there and you won't get any fish. Sometimes you don't get much but today was spot on.

Four-thirty in the morning and we were out on the water, just able to see from the lights on the beach and not a trace of the day starting out to sea. It's the best time to go fishing. Late afternoon can be good but usually the wind has picked up and it's too rough to go out. Early morning, the sea can be glassy. Not even a cat's paw – a tiny ripple – on the surface.

Grampa Jack is always looking for a good meal of snapper or kingfish, bream or flathead. And today we got snapper. Mine was by far the best, a ten-pounder at least. Gee, didn't he fight.

'Don't lose 'im, Nipper,' Grampa Jack was sayin' as the line was tuggin' every way and I'm tryin' to reel him in without getting me hands cut. 'Play 'im some. Tire 'im.'

I was getting tired myself but I kept going. I didn't want to lose such a good fish.

At last we got him up to the boat and Grampa Jack grabbed him and he was ours.

'Hooray! We're havin' snapper for our tea,' Grampa Jack said. 'Well done, Nip.'

We were back on the beach as the first light was growing on the horizon. There was still hardly anyone about as we put the boat in the shed. It was like we had Bondi to ourselves.

I was back home by eight o'clock with plenty of time

to get ready for school. No time for a couple of hours' sleep, but.

Grampa Jack said goodbye and then said, 'You did fine, Nipper.'

'Thanks, Grampa Jack.'

'There's not many I'd take out with me, but you know your way around a boat. And when you caught that big one, you didn't get too excited and sink us.'

'You're a good teacher, Grampa Jack.'

'You're a good learner, Nipper,' he said, and we both smiled. 'I enjoyed having you.'

Mum really enjoyed having some fillets that Grampa Jack brought around later. There was just enough for everyone's dinner because Grampa Jack reckons, 'Take no more 'n you need and leave the rest for next time.'

Saturday, 13 November 1937

Today the beach was beaut. Not only was it sunny and warm, with beautiful clean waves, but there were lamingtons as well. Now the weather is getting really nice, there's lots more people coming to the beach. Thousands and thousands of them. So Mum and the other ladies who are involved with the lifesaving clubs have started doing cake sales to help raise money. You could get a cup of tea and a slice of cake for sixpence, which is a bit dear, but everyone knows it's for a good cause.

There were lots of cakes: chocolate, sponge, orange, pavlova and cheesecake. But most of all, and my favourite, were the lamingtons. Mum had made heaps, so when we came by the stall we were allowed to have one. I wanted to have lamingtons for lunch, but Mum said that was no go.

They'll use the money they make to buy equipment for the club. They're looking to buy more surf reels, and they've started a special fund for a new surf boat for the Bondi club. The one they've got has been smashed and repaired so many times they're not sure it will hold together much longer.

The club has about three hundred and fifty members, mostly seniors, who are over the age of eighteen. Junior lifesavers are between sixteen and eighteen. A lot of the members are related to other members, like brothers, fathers and uncles. And when I'm a member, with Grampa Jack, it'll be grandfathers and grandsons. I think I mentioned, the beach inspectors are separate to the lifesavers. They're paid by the council and are on duty mainly through the week, making sure the beach is safe every single day. Officially, they have the weekend off, but most go to the beach anyway. That's when the lifesavers, all the locals and the weekenders, work as volunteers to take the pressure off the inspectors on the busy days, Saturday and Sunday.

Everything is very organised. Every day there's a beach patrol at Bondi and North Bondi (inspectors or lifesavers) with twelve members on duty at any one time. There's a morning patrol from six o'clock in the morning until one o'clock in the afternoon. Then there's a second patrol from one until six in the evening. The afternoon patrol is two hours shorter because it's often the busier of the two patrols. See, in the morning patrol, it's usually quiet for the first couple of hours. At six o'clock there aren't so many people, and most who swim at that time are locals and know what they're doing. There are more visitors on the beach in the afternoon, and that's when more people get into trouble.

Each patrol has at least two or three really good strong swimmers, who take out the belt. They tie a belt around their middle, or over one shoulder, with a line attached to it and swim out to whoever is in trouble. The morning patrol sets up a dozen or more reels all the way along the beach, because you never know where one is going to be needed. So no matter where an emergency happens, there's a surf reel ready.

When the afternoon patrol ends, they carry all the surf reels back to the clubhouse. Then, if there's time, they do some training, especially for the march past. Saturday and Sunday, after the beach patrols end, the march past teams, twenty men per team, practise their marching. It's great to see them, arms moving in unison, eyes straight ahead, all in step. Lots of people watch them and applaud, even though they're only practising. And always, the older blokes are teaching the younger ones the discipline required for the march past.

The seniors show the juniors the ropes. Like, they know the best ways to get out through the waves the fastest. You have to go out different ways depending on whether it's low tide or high tide. At low tide, when the water is shallow, you dive through each wave and stand up, dive and stand, like a porpoise, to get over the sand banks, being careful not to dive head first into the sand, which could result in a broken neck. When the tide's full, the banks are already submerged, so you get into deep water more quickly and as soon as you can, you start swimming.

Sunday, 21 November 1937

You know what, diary? It's a shame Mrs Kearsley and I don't get on. If we did, I'd thank her for getting me started writing in you. Dunno why, but I like putting in stuff about what's going on, even when not much is happening. Like today. Nothing happened, but it was still beaut.

Early mornings at Bondi are my favourite time, especially now the weather's warmed up. There's only a few people down on the beach or in the water. The sun is coming up and shimmering over the waves. Here and there the gulls are standing on the shore in little groups that look like they're having a meeting about something. They're only disturbed when the first surf patrol carries the surf reels down the beach, ready for the day's rescues. Once that's done, most of the lifesavers go for a quick swim. Some mornings, a couple of the lifesavers that are keen on boxing do a bit of sparring, with a ring

108

marked out in the sand. They reckon boxing on sand is good training for boxing in the ring: it gives your legs a good workout. They put on the gloves, box for a couple of rounds, then shake hands and dive into the water for another surf. The seagulls stand on the sand watching all this, and sometimes I do too.

A little later on, there's activity around the bathing Pavilion. It's usually open early for people to get changed for their early morning swim or have a shower afterwards. But soon the sun chairs are lined up outside the Pavilion and the surf-o-planes are all stacked up ready to be hired.

Then the upstairs is opened for people to come and play mini-golf. There are two ballrooms up there, but only the smaller one is used for dancing. The main ballroom is used for mini-golf, which is much more popular. You have to pay though, unlike Rose Cottage, where if the lifesavers that live there like you, you can play for free.

There are other places to play mini-golf around Bondi. A lot of people come to the beach and say, 'Oh, it's too cold to swim. Let's play mini-golf.' You didn't have to go to the beach to play mini-golf but that's what they do.

There are always problems with the Pavilion. It

keeps sinking. Grampa Jack reckons it's because it was built on a rubbish tip, but Dad says it was probably built on rotting sharks. Anyway, hardly a month goes by when they aren't shoring up part of it with cement and bricks and anything else they can find. They can't let it fall down. I don't reckon anyone could imagine Bondi without the Pavilion. Grampa Jack's probably right about the foundations but I like Dad's story better. Imagine a whole building sitting on the backs of hundreds of sharks.

As the day goes on, the busiest part of the beach is the bathing sheds, next to the Pavilion. They have thousands of lockers where people can get changed and lock up their clothes and valuables. For those who don't want to get changed in front of other people, there are three hundred cabins that they can rent. The women's sheds have even more cabins because more women don't want to be seen getting changed. After you get changed, you walk through the shower rooms and then down two tunnels, one for the men and one for the women, out to the piers and down to the beach.

People can hire bathing costumes at the Pavilion too. There isn't much difference between the men's and women's costumes. They both extend from neck to knee. Nearly every swimsuit is black. Men's and women's costumes, all black. The only thing that makes them different is if they have the lifesaving insignia or the Bondi Swimming Club letters. And they are all made of wool too. Fine wool that doesn't scratch or go out of shape when it gets wet.

Most lifesavers wear bathers that are like a vest. They leave most of their shoulders bare but have straps from their chest that cross on their back. They reckon they are better for diving through the waves, and the straps make sure your costume doesn't get pulled off by the water. Some wear swimming trunks without the straps, but with a belt that can be tightened for the same reason. You didn't want to be saving someone and end up wearing nothing, although there have been rescues where off-duty lifesavers have seen someone in trouble and stripped off to go in. It meant a little bit of embarrassment but it didn't matter if they saved a life.

Monday, 22 November 1937

Hey diary. This morning, early, I went to the beach, dived

in, then swam four hundred yards down to the Pavilion. It's easier when you kind of swim with the waves, rather than against them. Sometimes you have to delay a stroke or kick, just for a moment. Sometimes you have to be a bit quicker. If you do though it's much easier. You don't waste energy fighting the waves. When I got to the Pavilion, I body surfed in, touched the sand, turned and went straight back out, fifty yards or more, to the back of the breakers, then fifty yards sidestroke back, like I was rescuing someone.

Bronze medallion? Just about.

'Reckon I should stop making you toast, Nipper,' Dad said when I got home. 'I'm sure you're growing bigger every day. You're starting to get shoulders like Grampa Jack.'

'Just keep 'em comin', Dad,' I said with a grin as I devoured my sixth slice.

Tuesday, 23 November 1937

Rainy day today, diary. I don't like the rain much – cold and wet and no good for the beach. Rachel, though, she loves it. This morning she put on her mackintosh, sou'wester and gumboots and splashed her way to school through every puddle she could find.

'Everyone is dressed the same, in black. We are all equal,' she said.

She can be a bit strange sometimes but that's okay. Damo is a bit weird sometimes too. For example, he likes body surfing when the waves are dumpers. As the wave rolls over and heads straight down, he tucks into a ball and gets tumbled head over heels while sandy water is spurting up his nose, in his ears, everywhere. When he comes up, he looks like a drowned cat. Except he's laughing.

I reckon I'm the only normal one in our gang.

Friday, 26 November 1937

'David,' Rachel asked me on the way home today, 'what does *Nipper* mean?'

Rachel is getting really good at English, but there are still things she doesn't understand. To get better at it, she reads everything she can get from the library and listens to the radio all the time. Whenever I go around to her place, she and her mum, and sometimes her dad, are listening to education talks or radio theatre or some of the serials that are on. My favourite radio programs are the quiz shows, especially when you can beat the contestants to get the answers. Dad is really good at that because he's super smart. Rachel reckons the radio is also a good way to learn all the funny expressions Australians have. But one word she's never heard used is 'nipper'.

'A nipper is like a crab,' I explained. 'You know those ones with big claws? They can really hurt. But the little ones can only give you a little nip, so they're called nippers. I got called Nipper because I'm littler than my big brother, Jamie. I've been called Nipper all me life.'

'Can anyone call you Nipper?'

'I think so,' I said. 'But mostly it's me friends.'

'Can I call you Nipper?'

'Well, I like how you call me David,' I said, 'except you say *Davit*, but you can call me Nipper too.'

Saturday, 27 November 1937

Mum and Dad, me and Damo, Josie and Rachel and Grampa Jack were all down on the beach this afternoon when yet another swimmer got into trouble. The lifesavers went in with the belt and line, and Grampa Jack went to help. The lifesaver with the belt got to the person, an older woman. He got hold of her from behind, held her head up out of the water, and the men on the reel started winding in the line. Unfortunately, when they got this woman to the beach, just near us, she wasn't breathing. A big crowd gathered around, as they always do, while the lifesavers tried to revive her.

'They're using the Schafer method,' Damo explained to Rachel. 'That'll get her right.'

All the Bondi lifesavers are trained in the Schafer method, which was worked out by an English doctor. They position the person on their front, then press down on their back to expel the water from their lungs and help them start breathing. There are some people who reckon you can use a method where you put your mouth on the drowned person's mouth to blow air directly into their lungs, but at Bondi they all use the Schafer method. I think it's because the people they're reviving usually have water in their lungs, and getting rid of that is the first thing to worry about.

Anyway, Grampa Jack and the others were taking turns pushing on this woman's back when eventually she gave a cough, threw up some water, then started gasping for air. Everyone started cheering, because it's like magic when someone who's almost dead comes back to life like that.

Everyone was patting them on the back and saying well done, but the lifesavers just went back on patrol. A couple of them stayed with the woman, waiting for the ambulance to arrive and take her to the hospital, where they'd watch over her in case she had a bad turn.

Grampa Jack came back over to us and sat down like he hadn't really done anything. Of course, all us kids thought he was the best, a real-life hero. It's one of the strange things about living at Bondi. You're just having a family outing, when suddenly someone nearby is in danger of losing their life, and your grampa just walks over, saves them and walks back. All along the beach, there's these blokes who save people every day of the week. And no one makes much of a fuss. It's just a pat on the back, maybe, and 'Well done, mate'. If they ran into a burning building instead of the surf, their names would be in all the papers. Mind you, everyone around Bondi knows all about them. When they walk along the promenade on Sunday evenings in their lifesavers' blazers, everyone says hello to them. We're proud of them. And all us kids want to be them.

And yeah, I do go on about them a bit, but that's the way it is.

Monday, 29 November 1937

I passed my exam. Actually, I did really well. I got the second-best mark in the class for the English part of the test. Rachel got the second-best mark in maths. Guess who beat Rachel for maths? Damo! He was really surprised. Now he's wondering if he's too smart to be a fireman. This other girl who is really quiet, Cheryl Talty, got the best mark in English but I didn't mind too much about that. I was surprised I did so well, although I reckon I have a secret weapon when it comes to English. And that's you, diary. I really like writing about all the stuff that happens, and I reckon it might be making a difference. Even Mrs Kearsley muttered something about 'finally realising your potential'. Couldn't say 'well done' but, like she did all the other kids. Mum and Dad and Grampa Jack all said 'we told you so'.

Tuesday, 30 November 1937

Rachel was in a bit of a mood at school today. Turned out there was something in the paper that she read. There's this war in Spain that her country, Germany, is involved in, and apparently a whole lot of Spanish people just got killed by the Germans. She said there were thousands of them. I didn't really understand why that was bad, but it seems people like her family don't like what her country is doing. And what happened at this place was one of the worst things it's done.

'They keep getting away with it,' Rachel said.

Wednesday, 1 December 1937

And now it really is summer. I love these long warm days, and it's only a little over two weeks and the summer school holidays will begin. Weeks and weeks of going to the beach. And Jamie will be home for Christmas, at least for a few days, so everything will be just like it used to be.

Every day now when I go to the beach I can swim my four hundred and do my fifties. It's still quite hard, but a lot easier than it was. So now I've got a new challenge. More than four hundred. As far as I can get.

Actually, what I want is to swim a length of Bondi.

Thursday, 2 December 1937

Saw that old Aboriginal fella Arthur again today. Just up the road, near where the rock carvings are. Now that I know him (well, I met him once), it's funny, but I've been seeing him about quite a bit. I reckon he may have always been there but I just haven't noticed until now. Rachel has seen him a few times too. He doesn't say hello, but we see him and we reckon he sees us.

Saturday, 4 December 1937

Yep, it's summer all right. There's been north-easterlies blowing for the last week, and now there are bluebottles washing up on the beach. Bondi doesn't get a lot because it faces more to the south, but some still drift in. One of them got me. Gee, it hurt. Sometimes you can get the sting off by rubbing it with sand, but this was right across my chest, and I couldn't get rid of it. I ran up the beach, trying not to cry from the pain, and found Mum. As I've said before, she has everything you could ever need at the beach in her big bag, and so she pulled out a little bottle of white vinegar. She rubbed some on the sting, and almost like magic it disappeared. After a couple of minutes I felt better and wanted to go back in the water.

She said, 'Be careful.'

And I said, 'Righto,' while running back down to the water.

Monday, 13 December 1937

Mrs Kearsley was actually nice to me today. What a surprise!

It's the last week of school and for some kids it's the last week of school forever. And now the Primary Final is all done, the school year is pretty much over. So this week we're really just tidying up our desks and the schoolroom because it's going to be closed up for weeks until next year.

Anyway, Mrs Kearsley made a little speech about how well we'd worked during the year. She wished everyone well with their future, whether at school or out working somewhere. She congratulated Cheryl on her results in the Primary Final, and Rachel and Damo. Then she said to me, 'I think David surprised us all with what he can do when he applies himself. I think you even surprised yourself.'

All I could do was blush.

Friday, 17 December 1937

No more schoolyard, no more books, NO MORE
teachers' dirty looks. Yes! School holidays. No more Mrs
Kearsley, ever. Even after the hols, I only have to go to
school until my thirteenth birthday in March, and then I
can leave any time I want. Except everyone reckons that's
a no go, especially Mum and Dad.

Tomorrow we're putting the Christmas tree up. And
Mum's already starting baking things, in between going
to the beach.

Saturday, 18 December 1937

Now the holidays have begun, there are even more people
coming to Bondi. Today there were tens of thousands of
them. In the morning, every few minutes a double tram
would pull up and two hundred or two hundred and fifty
people would spill out. The trams were carrying as many
people as could fit on. It went on like that all day. In the

afternoon, there were huge crowds waiting for a tram to go home, although no one seemed to mind. They'd all spent a day at the beach and there wasn't much that could spoil their good mood.

It'll be a bit different tomorrow. Because it's Sunday, a lot of people will stay on to watch the band, then go for a milkshake, and take a late tram home. Some people won't go home at all. School holidays mean that lots of people, especially country people, spend the hot months of summer by the sea. Speaking of which, Jamie will be coming home for Christmas soon. I'm not sure exactly when but it can only be a couple of days away.

Sunday, 19 December 1937

Everything is the same, but everything is different, better. In the rotunda, the Bondi Beach Band played from seven until nine. We promenaded as we always do. There were heaps more people, holidaymakers already. Grampa Jack and the other lifesavers stood out because they all wore their North Bondi and Bondi lifesavers' blazers. Everyone admired them. After that we went to Powell's for a milkshake and then home. We didn't stay up too late because Dad has to go to work tomorrow. But us kids know we can get up, on a Monday, and be in the water before the sun comes up. And stay there as long as we want. There's nothing like the feeling that the summer holidays are stretching out forever. Six whole weeks!

Reckon I'll be swimming lengths of Bondi by the end of the hols for sure. I'm already three-quarters of the way there, and every day I feel like I'm getting stronger. You can actually see the muscles growing. Mum reckons she's got to take me shopping because I'm getting too big for my clothes.

Dad said, 'Maybe save some money and just get him new bathers. That's all he ever wears these days.'

Monday, 20 December 1937

Gee, it was a bit of a wake-up today. First day of actual school holidays, as in, not the weekend, and for most of the Bondi kids we could all look forward to weeks and weeks of being able to do whatever we wanted – swimming and sand and sunshine and fishing and picture shows and everything for longer than we can imagine. But it wasn't that way for the kids who finished school. For them it should have been even better. No more school, ever! But some had already got jobs, and instead of holidays they had to work. After all, the week before Christmas is a busy time for a lot of places, especially as it's the start of holiday time at Bondi. Other kids had holidays only until after Christmas, then they were starting work. And then some kids had left school but didn't have jobs. Damo and I saw Percy Mason up on Campbell Parade when we were cashing in a bottle we found. He didn't want to come for a swim. He said he was going from shop to shop seeing if they had anything he could do.

'Me brother reckons there might be something at the factory where he works, out Chullora way, in a couple of months,' he said. 'In the meantime, if you hear of anythin'.'

He was two-thirds of the way along the road, and everyone had said 'no go'.

The big Depression may have been over but Dad reckons that for every ten people there's one still out of work after nearly a decade. It used to be one in three, but I still didn't think much of Percy's chances. No holidays for him. He had a full-time occupation finding a job.

After we left him I thought about my job with

the greengrocer. I wasn't doing it because I needed the money. But if I left school, it'd be different. I might end up like Percy, trudging around Bondi or going to Chullora, some place miles out west. Or like Jamie, up there in the Hunter Valley, missing the beach, and us, although he'll be home this week. Talk about casting a shadow.

The waves? They were holiday waves. Easy to catch, the water warm. We stayed in swimming for hours.

Tuesday, 21 December 1937

Rachel, Damo and me went over to South Head to try and see that old bloke Arthur, but he wasn't at his house over on the edge of Sydney Harbour. We went for a bit of a search along the shore, thinking he might be fishing or something. No sign. The harbour looked beaut but. There were a few boats sailing up and down and big ships coming and going. Off in the distance we could see the tall buildings of the city and the white AWA antenna, the tallest thing in the city, soaring over all of them. What's amazing, though, is the Harbour Bridge is even taller. It looks a bit strange, actually, this giant bridge that's bigger than anything else around.

Thursday, 23 December 1937

Jamie's home! He's sleeping in the pullout bed beside me while I write this, although it's not very late. But he was up at five milking cows before he caught the train down to Sydney to spend Christmas with us. I only saw him a couple of months ago, but he's grown taller and a lot stronger. It's all that hay he carries around, he reckons. I wonder if I'll be as big and strong as he is when I'm fourteen.

Friday, 24 December 1937

Hey diary, big day on Sydney Harbour today. A Catalina flying boat landed at Rose Bay. It was this huge black plane that could land on water, then it had wheels so it could drive up on to a big concrete platform that they've built right down into the water. The landing was at the new flying boat base, which is where people can fly all over the world in the new Qantas Empire flying boats if they're rich enough. But the Catalinas are war planes, part of the plan to defend Sydney in case of attack. I'm not really sure who is going to do that. It's hard to imagine Germany coming to the other side of the world to attack us, but the armed forces are getting ready anyway. And Rachel reckons anything is possible with that Adolf Hitler fella.

'He makes war with everyone he doesn't like,' she said. 'Even Germans like us, because of our religion.'

Mum and Mrs Freeman took all us kids over to see the show. There were naval ships and flypasts, and then the Catalina came in flying low and did some big circles around the harbour. It was slow and huge and looked like it was going to fall out of the sky at any moment. And being black it looked pretty sinister. The landing on the water was fabulous. It flew around the city and then came in low past Darling Point. It touched down just past Point Piper and there was this huge plume of spray on both sides of it. It skimmed along for a little while then slowed down really quickly and settled deeper in the water. You could sort of tell when it stopped being a plane and sank down and started being a boat.

Damo and I thought it was beaut but Rachel didn't like it.

'What if enemy has planes like this?' she said.

'You're a long way from all that now, dear,' Mum said.

'How far can that thing fly?' Rachel asked.

Mum said she didn't know.

Then Mrs Freeman said, 'I'm sure Papa wouldn't bring us so far if he didn't think we'd be safe.'

Saturday, 25 December 1937

Hey diary. Merry Christmas! And it really is. I got my very own bike. It's a beauty. A Speedwell, three gears, painted blue. It really flies, and there are some great hills around Bondi to ride it down. Riding up is the hard part. We had a wonderful Christmas lunch. Jamie was there, of course, and Grampa Jack, and Mum invited the Freemans too. Apparently they don't usually celebrate Christmas because of their religion, but they came to lunch anyway and had a great time.

The best bit was that Mum and Mrs Freeman decided that, even though the Freemans gave Rachel presents during Hanukkah – that's a Jewish celebration near Christmas time – us kids could exchange presents anyway. So Josie, Jamie and I got to give Rachel her very own medium-size surf-o-plane! Rachel gave Josie a small surf-o-plane and she gave me a book that's just been published in England. Her dad got it from a shop in the city that specialises in the latest books from overseas. It's called *The Hobbit,* by J. R. R. Tolkien. Rachel's already bagsed reading it after I've finished. I think it might make a good change from all the *Tarzan* books she borrows. Rachel didn't forget Jamie either, and gave him a beautiful stockman's pocket knife with all kinds of useful attachments.

Sunday, 26 December 1937

Today is called Boxing Day because it used to be the day when servants were given a day off by their masters and a box full of presents and treats. It also used to be the day when there were lots of boxing tournaments. Down at the beach, Don and Clem, two of the lifesavers, had a bit of a bout, but that was the only boxing on Bondi today. Other than that it was just another holiday like any other. Lots and lots of people at the beach. Every few minutes, someone was being rescued or helped back between the flags, even though the waves were pretty gentle, mostly chop from a nor-easter.

Jamie reckons it feels strange to be back in Bondi.

'Too crowded,' he said, when we were trying to find Mum and Dad on the beach, and our towels, even though they were at our usual spot near the north pier. 'I'm used to me and Uncle Neville and a few cows. Not these thousands of people.'

He reckons the next time he comes down he might go to Maroubra, where it's quieter. That's a beach a fair bit down the coast from Bondi. There's nothing much there except sand dunes and tussocks, and a bit of an old shipwreck.

'It's the middle of nowhere,' I said. 'You might as well go swimming in the Wollombi Brook.'

That was the little river that wound past Uncle Neville's dairy farm.

'I miss the surf,' Jamie said.

'We miss you,' I said.

'Yeah,' he said. 'I know.'

We found Mum and Dad and headed towards them. Then Jamie grabbed my arm and stopped me.

'Promise me something, Nip,' he said. 'Whatever you do, you'll stay at school.'

He couldn't be serious.

'I'm not promisin' nuthin,' I said. 'If I get a chance, I'm gone.'

Not that I entirely believed it, but that's what you

say when you think it might be how things will turn out.

'Really, Nipper,' Jamie said. 'I love bein' on the farm, but if I had it all to do again, I'd do it different.'

'Why's that?'

'I'm startin' to understand what I had to give up to get what I wanted.'

That afternoon, Jamie and I (and Rachel, Damo and Josie) swam and surf-o-planed until the sun went down. Sometimes that's the best time of the day, when the froth is all sparkling with the setting sun and some bits shine silver and others shine gold. When the water's warm you just want to keep swimming, at least until the shark fishermen start baiting up. I couldn't help thinking Jamie was making the most of it because he's going back to the farm tomorrow.

'Them cows won't milk 'emselves,' he said, and he sounded like a real farmer, like Uncle Neville.

Monday, 27 December 1937

Hey diary. Went with Jamie to Central Station to say goodbye. He'll be back milking his cows tonight. He was at me a bit more too.

He shook my hand and said, 'Make me proud, little brother.'

It was a strange thing to say. Does he think I'll one day be as good at anything as he is?

Sat next to Bea Miles on the tram back to Bondi. Well, she sat next to me. She's a big woman, and she smells a bit, but not as much as Bondi Mary. She wanted to know all about me, not that there's much to tell, and turns out she knows Grampa Jack and a few other lifesavers. She reckoned they were all gentlemen, which I guess is true.

Then she made up a game and insisted I play. It was who could count the most Fords and who could count the most Chevrolets. She said I could count Fords and I was sure I'd see more but she had eyes like a hawk. She saw Chevies everywhere, and it was only when she said I could count Ford trucks as well that I started to catch up. On the run down to Bondi, we were equal, on forty-two each. Then we went past the police station.

'All the cars are Fords!' I shouted. There were four of them. 'Forty-six!'

Bea was counting the Chevies parked at the beach. There were three. I won by one car. I think she let me win.

Tuesday, 28 December 1937

Funny thing at the beach today. There was this little kid, maybe only three or four, and he hated sand. He wanted to go with his mum and dad down to the water but he would not, Would Not, WOULD NOT step on the sand. They're saying, 'Come on, just walk', but he refused and cried and carried on. So his dad had to pick him up and carry him to the water. He played in the shallows with all the other kids, but when it was time to go back to his towel, he wouldn't go on the sand again. His dad had to carry him back. Then there he was, sitting on his towel, as far from the edges as he could get, saying, 'I don't like the sand.' Mind you, it does stick to your feet, and if you're from the country and aren't used to it, it might seem strange. But of all the things to be scared of, sand is a new one.

I told Grampa Jack about it on the way back from the Diggers. He thought it was a good story.

'Not like yours, Grampa Jack,' I said. 'Yours are the best.'

'I see how you're developing your powers of observation,' he said. 'You'll match me soon enough.

Now did I ever tell you about the time a whale came up beside me dinghy when I was fishin'?'

We both knew he'd told me a hundred times. The whale came up with a mighty blow, all black on top and white underneath. Ten times the length of the dinghy, if he was an inch. Then the whale stopped and looked at Grampa Jack with a big round eye. And Grampa Jack thought if he was going to smash his dinghy to splinters, he'd have done so by now, so he tipped his cap to the whale. And with that the whale sounded and swam right under the boat. Grampa Jack watched him go, and all was well until the tail went by. It gave a mighty swish that spun the dinghy around twice. When Grampa Jack stopped spinning, the whale was gone.

I'd love to be able to tell stories like Grampa Jack. Even better, like J. R. R. Tolkien. I've been reading that book I got for Christmas. It's full of dwarves and elves and ogres and adventures for the hero, who's the hobbit. I'm almost halfway through and I'm wishing the story wouldn't end. I'd love to write a book like that. Actually, any kind of book. Wouldn't it be great to live at Bondi, sitting at a window overlooking the beach and writing stories for a living? Who knows, maybe one day.

I'm doing it now, except it's a diary. Sorry, diary.

Saturday, 1 January 1938

The first day of a new year. There was a party for our street in the park on Ben Buckler last night and us kids were allowed to stay up late, then Mum brought us home to bed and she and Dad and Grampa Jack stayed up with the neighbours to welcome in the new year. It was a public holiday today, but it was the weekend anyway, and while it was quiet on the beach in the morning, it was really busy during the afternoon. Grampa Jack slept in but he was on duty with the lifesavers in the afternoon.

'Always busy on New Year's Day,' he said. 'People still tired after a big night out. They think a swim will freshen 'em up. It never does.'

Tuesday, 4 January 1938

Grampa Jack came tapping at my window at four this morning. Nice fishing in the early dawn. Glassy sea, almost no waves. Red and purple and then gold to the east. A couple of good fish in the boat and then home for breakfast as the sleepyheads were just getting up.

'Come on,' Grampa Jack said to Josie, who was still yawning. 'The day's half over.'

Later on, down at the beach, Damo and Rachel and me were out on the back bank, taking turns on Rachel's surf-o-plane, when the beach inspectors rescued a bloke and his young son who were out there with us.

We were all having fun catching not very big waves when these two fellas came out and said to this bloke, 'We're here to rescue you.'

He was completely surprised. 'Do I need rescuing?'

'Can you swim?' they asked him.

'Not very well,' the bloke admitted. 'And my boy even less.'

It turned out that while he'd been out there, the tide had been coming in, and the channel between the sand bank and the beach had filled up. It was too deep for them to get back across.

This bloke only noticed when they pointed it out to him.

'What about them?' the man said, pointing at us.

'They're locals,' one of the beach inspectors said, and gave me a wink. 'They can save 'emselves.'

The man was amazed when he realised he really did need help getting back across the channel. After the beach inspectors helped him and his boy get back to the shore, he went up to his locker and came back and gave each of 'em five shillings! I know because neither of them felt right taking money for doing their job and they gave the money to me!

'Give it to your mum,' they said, 'for the surf boat fund.'

Wednesday, 5 January 1938

Bondi. One length. In at the northern end, out at the southern end. I'm probably the only twelve-year-old in Bondi who can swim it, then 'rescue' someone after. It really felt like I'd achieved something.

I'm feeling pretty proud of myself but I'm still wary of telling anyone. It's not that I'm afraid someone will say 'you're not good enough'. I know what I can do now and nothing anyone says can change that. And I don't think I'd care anyway. I just really enjoy swimming when it's just me and the waves. It's the only time of the day when I'm by myself. And when your head is under water, no one can tell you what to do.

Thursday, 6 January 1938

Grampa Jack says it's all hands on deck tomorrow. The annual Bondi surf carnival is on this weekend and there's lots to be done to get the beach ready for all the events. All us kids and all the available mums and anyone else who can spare a hand are being press-ganged into helping.

Friday, 7 January 1938

I'm exhausted. Everyone is exhausted. We've fenced off areas for events, for all the surf boats for visiting clubs, put up marquees, tables for officials to handle entries and events and trophies, a PA system, signs telling visitors where everything is and on and on. Surf boats started arriving after lunch and we had to show them where to go. Everyone was busy until it got dark. But we're ready.

Saturday, 8 January 1938

What a great day. There were hundreds of competitors on the beach and thousands of spectators for the events that were running all day. Everyone worked non-stop.

Rachel, Damo, Josie and I were running messages for much of the day but we did get to watch some of the events. Everyone who could stop, stopped for the march past. That's the main event, when lifesaving club after club marches in perfect step, in their immaculate club swimming costumes and swimming caps, carrying a surf reel behind their flagbearer, who holds the club banner proudly aloft. Everyone clapped and cheered, there were newspaper photographers taking pictures, and there were even people from Cinetone making a film for the movie news.

The weather was sunny and the waves were what Bondi does best – a good clean break with the occasional bigger wave to test out the competitors. The only interruption to proceedings was during the rescue race. A shark swam under the four 'patients' waiting to be rescued from a buoy two hundred yards off shore. A surf boat raised the alarm and picked up the patients but the beltmen swimming out got a bit of a surprise when they suddenly got a yank on the line and next thing they were being reeled back to the beach quick smart. No one got bitten, and all the shore events continued until they were sure the shark was gone.

Bondi came second in the march past, beaten by their old rivals, Manly. Bob Newbiggin from Newcastle won the junior swimming race and the belt race. He's just sixteen, but everyone reckons he's going to be one of the best. Our Aub won the swimming event. He's a real champion. Bondi won the main event, the surf boat race. The boat was getting pretty knocked about but we've got a good crew, and with a bit of local knowledge they managed to come from behind to catch a good wave that carried them into the lead. The roar from the crowd when they hit the beach drowned out the surf. What a superb day.

Now Grampa Jack says this was just the dress rehearsal. Bondi is hosting a special surf carnival in a month's time as part of Australia's celebrations for one hundred and fifty years of settlement. The celebrations have got a really funny name that would be hard to spell except there's all these posters going up to advertise the big event: the sesquicentenary. Grampa Jack reckons the Sesquicentenary Surf Carnival is going to be huge. There's even lifesavers coming from overseas.

Sunday, 9 January 1938

This Sunday night at Bondi everyone was out celebrating because Bondi had done well at the surf carnival. Nearly all the locals were on the promenade. Everyone was dressed up, and there were a few people from other surf clubs who'd stayed to be part of the festival atmosphere. They all stood out in their club blazers, and everyone was congratulating winning competitors. Even lifesavers who hadn't won anything were treated like they were special.

I so much want to be one of them. It doesn't matter who you are – when you put on that blazer, you're a lifesaver. There's all kinds of people in the surf club: lawyers and doctors, police, council workers, carpenters, mechanics, even builders from when they constructed the North Bondi Surf Club in the early 1930s, but what sets them apart is being a lifesaver.

Meanwhile, back on the promenade, there were so many people stopping to talk about the weather, the carnival, fundraising for the surf club and all sorts of things that one length up and down meeting people was enough for the whole evening.

Afterwards, ice creams. Up on Campbell Parade all the milk bars were packed. Dad and I queued up at

Powell's, our favourite place. While we were waiting, I looked through a door that led out the back. I noticed Percy Mason, from school, was working in the kitchen. I caught his eye and he gave me a smile. He looked a lot happier than when I'd last seen him. Then he came over.

'G'day Nipper,' he said.

'How long you been workin' here?' I asked.

'Just after Christmas,' he said. 'I kept comin' back and askin'. Eventually Mr Powell said yeah, just so I would stop askin'. Imagine, me workin' at Powell's. All the ice cream and fish and chips I can eat.'

'Best job in the world, I reckon,' I said.

Dad burst out laughing. 'He has to work for his ice cream,' he said. 'All you have to do is go on and on that you're starving.'

Monday, 10 January 1938

I got a bit of a swimming lesson today. I went for my morning length of the beach but as I was going along, I was thinking about Bob Newbiggin and how fast he swam to win the junior swimming race. I started trying to swim faster. I did the first half of the beach much quicker than I normally do but then I started feeling really tired. It was like I'd used all the strength I needed to do a whole length in the first half. I had to give up three-quarters of the way down the beach. Two lessons, actually: don't go too fast and don't try to be Bob Newbiggin when you're still only twelve.

Wednesday, 12 January 1938

There was a bunch of young English sailors on the beach today. You can tell them easily from everyone else. They're so white while everyone else is tanned. They were from one of the ships that trade back and forth between Australia and England, on the other side of the world. There was a bit of a tradition for sailors for their first time to Australia. They had to go for a surf at the famous Bondi Beach. They'd get off the tram, walk on to the beach and dive straight into the water. No thought about flags, or rips, or dangerous surf. Straight in. Some ended up right out the back with the sharks, wondering if they'd drown or get eaten.

The beach inspectors went out to rescue them and some didn't even know they were in trouble. They were having a great time, their first experience of surf at Bondi.

Actually, there were three things sailors had to do when they came to Sydney: Bondi, the Blue Mountains and Taronga Zoo. If they had three days' leave, they were the top three. A day trip to experience each one.

That reminds me of another of Grampa Jack's stories. He saved one young Englishman once who got into a rip going out the back, started drowning, and was unconscious by the time Grampa Jack got him to the beach. Not breathing. So they used the Schafer method to resuscitate him and he came around, but he wasn't very well, so the ambulance took him to St Vincent's Hospital. That night, Grampa rang to find out if the young man was on the mend. The hospital checked and said he was doing well. A few days later, a letter came for Grampa Jack from the fellow, who was a cook on a ship. It was posted in Melbourne, the ship's next port of call. The young man had heard that Grampa Jack rang the hospital and was grateful that he cared enough to ask after him. He put a pound note in with the letter to say thank you. Of course Grampa Jack donated it to the lifesaving club.

Thursday, 13 January 1938

Rachel got into trouble today because she was skipping with Josie and one of her shoes, her good shoes, split open. Her mother kept going on about how much the shoes cost. EIGHTEEN SHILLINGS! EIGHTEEN SHILLINGS! The whole street knew how much they cost. But it's summer. Who needs shoes? Half the kids at Bondi Public don't even have any.

Friday, 14 January 1938

I wish summer would go on forever. When we aren't swimming, we're either going swimming or coming back from swimming. That or we're on the lookout for soft-drink bottles. If you return them you get a penny, or the equivalent in lollies, or if you gathered a few, you could buy a hamburger.

Sometimes we'd spot a surf-o-plane that someone had left lying around. They cost sixpence a half-hour to hire from Mr McDonald, so if you found one lying around you could get a free ride, at least for a little while. Surf-o-planes were the best for shooting the surf. You could catch waves easier and you could turn, at least most of the time. If you caught the wrong wave you could just get dumped and then you wouldn't know where you were.

Now that Rachel is getting better as a swimmer and has her own surf-o-plane, she's out in the water with us all the time. What's even more fun than riding a surf-o-plane is when you and a friend have one each and you can surf along together. You can even try to bump each other off, especially if it's Damo.

Rachel and Josie have also joined the Bondi Ladies Swimming Club. The women of Bondi, because they couldn't join the lifesavers, started their own club. Mum's been a member forever. The women run races in the ocean pool every Saturday. Rachel doesn't do very well in her races but she loves the club. She especially loves her bathers with the letters BLSC on them. A lot of visitors mistakenly think it stands for Bondi Life Saving Club. I'm sure a lot of the BLSC women know that too.

Saturday, 15 January 1938

Another great day at Bondi. We spent the morning swimming, then in the afternoon we went to the pictures. There was a choice of movies at Kings or Six-Ways or

Bondi Road. *Tarzan's Revenge* was on at Bondi Road. We made a real racket, although there was a big message that came up on the screen before the features that said: *Silence Is Golden*. We didn't know much about that.

After we'd spent hours at the pictures in the dark, we came outside and the sun really hurt our eyes. At least for a little while. We headed right back to the beach and had a last scan for lemonade bottles or unattended surf-o-planes, then had a swim before going home to pester Mum and Dad, then Rachel's mum and dad, then Damo's mum and dad, for fish and chips.

If that wasn't enough, there was a movie being screened at the beach this evening as well. You could sit out on deckchairs in the open and watch. Us kids got to see it for free. We managed to sneak in under the canvas fence and get a good possie up the front.

Monday, 17 January 1938

Hey diary. I came upon that old fella Arthur today. I was off riding my bike on my own up along the cliffs at Dover Heights and saw him looking at the view.

I wasn't sure if I should bother him, but he turned

round and raised his hand to show that he'd seen me.

'G'day, Arthur,' I said.

'G'day, Nipper,' Arthur said back. 'I see you and your friends been round my place.'

'We thought we'd come for another visit but we missed you. And then when we've seen you, you haven't said hello or nothin'.'

'I know,' he said. 'I like keepin' to meself.'

By now we were walking along the cliff top, me just pushing my bike along.

'Suppose the last thing you want is us kids hangin' around?' I said.

He didn't answer. Instead, he asked me a question.

'Enjoying your holidays?'

I was about to say 'of course' when something stopped me.

'You know what?' I said. 'It's fun but it feels strange. Like it might be the last summer that's just like this.'

'Ah,' was all he said.

We walked a bit further through the heath and then came out on to an open space of bare rock. From there you could see all the way up the coast to Sydney Heads and down the coast towards Botany.

Not far away was the Macquarie Lighthouse.

'Do you know this place, Nipper?'

I shook my head.

'In the old days, this is where the old people brought the young boys, twelve years old, just like you, and they had a big ceremony. After that ceremony, the boys became men.'

'When they were twelve?'

'That's right,' he said. 'After that, everything changes.'

'Just with a ceremony,' I said, a bit disbelieving. 'I wish it was that easy.'

'It's never easy,' Arthur said with a laugh, 'I know. I've got the scars to prove it.'

Tuesday, 18 January 1938

I didn't tell anyone about seeing Arthur yesterday. Except for writing it in here. Dunno why. It was a bit of a strange conversation, and afterwards, he went his way and I went mine. I rode home, did my vegie deliveries and walked home with Grampa Jack.

And now there's this cloud starting to lurk on the horizon. School is less than two weeks away. Mum mentioned getting new shoes today, and I got that strange sad feeling that another summer was ending. And going back to school? For a lot of boys at Bondi Public, turning thirteen is what makes them men. Then they go and get jobs.

All day long we mucked around like we usually do. Rachel, Damo and me went exploring in a few building sites, looking for any drink bottles that the builders might have left behind. Managed to get a couple of good bits of wood for a billy cart. Most of us kids already have billy carts but you can't ignore good bits of wood when you see them. For repairs when you crash.

We went for a swim in the afternoon then we came home and played a few games. Josie insisted we play little kids' games: chasings, then statues, then O'Grady Says. It was only when Damo and I started getting bored that we played a game we wanted: Cowboys and Indians. Damo loves being the Indian. 'Me scalpum paleface,' was his favourite phrase. Then the iceman came around, and as usual, everything stopped while we tried to get some chips of ice to suck. The poor iceman, with about ten kids around him going, 'Please mister, please mister'. And it was like that in every street he went to. When it's hot there's nothing like getting a nice chip of ice to suck.

The ice works are over in Murriverie Road. The iceman does his rounds to deliver ice every couple of days so the fridge stays cool. He has these special tongs for carrying the big blocks of ice into the house but when he uses them he often chips bits of ice off. They'd soon melt anyway, so at nearly every house he goes to he has some chips of ice for us kids. He brought the ice in a little flat-top truck, with a tarpaulin over the ice so it wouldn't melt. At least not much.

I love the way the ice looks when it's tipped out of the can, about three feet long and like a big piece of solid glass. There are bubbles and what look like white splinters inside. It's like a magic world that over the next couple of days will slowly melt away. I like to look at the ice in the fridge, but Mum gets cranky if I keep opening the door. Still, when the old block is taken out, mostly melted, I get to have it and watch the last of it disappear.

There are plenty of other people who do deliveries as well – the milkman, the baker, rabbitohs (who sell rabbits) and knife sharpeners – but our favourite is the iceman. We still pester the other deliverymen just in case they have something we can get as a treat. The only person we leave alone is the dunny man.

Wednesday, 19 January 1938

For a special treat, Mum and Rachel's mum took us to the Ice Palais in Woolloomooloo today to go ice skating. Josie and I were keen to try, but the ice was so slippery we couldn't go more than a few feet before we fell over. We went around the edge of the ice holding on to a rail. Even then we were struggling to keep our balance. Meanwhile Rachel, who I always thought wasn't very good at anything, was gliding and turning and even doing little spins. After a while we just stood and watched. Eventually, she came over.

'You're really good,' said Josie, and even she sounded surprised.

'Not really,' Rachel said, 'but everyone in Germany skates, at least through the winter, when everything freezes.'

She took us by the hands and helped us slowly venture out on the ice. I wasn't really comfortable holding hands with a girl, but it helped to keep my balance and after a little while I got a bit of confidence. Before I was ready, Rachel let me go. My arms flailed while I tried to stay upright, but I managed not to fall. I went right across the ice and ran straight into a wall because I didn't know how to stop or turn. Rachel was already over with Josie, helping her. After a while, Josie was gliding beside Rachel, saying 'not too fast, not too fast'. By the time we left, she was saying 'faster, faster'.

Saturday, 22 January 1938

The beach was really, really crowded today. The school holidays are about to end, and it's like everyone is cramming in as much swimming as they can before they have to go back to wherever they came from. It was so crowded that we went over to Tamarama to see if it was quieter.

There's not much of a beach there but it's sheltered from the winds, so it's good for sunbaking. Trouble is, if the waves are even a little bit big it's too rough in the water and they don't allow swimming. Sure enough, it was too rough, and there were rips everywhere. It was the same over at Bronte, the next beach along. There was almost always a rip there and the waves were mostly dumpers.

So first you'd get pounded by a wave, then you'd get dragged out to sea. There were a few fellas, though, who loved Bronte. They were the surfriders, who ride these giant boards made of plywood, and the Bronte rip made it easy for them to get out to where the big waves were. They jumped in the rip, got carried out, then surfed the waves back in. They still had to deal with the dumpers when they came back to shore, but they reckoned it was worth it.

We headed back to Bondi and got there just in time for all the commotion when the police caught a gang of thieves on the beach. There were people running everywhere.

You see, because there are so many people at Bondi, it's tempting for thieves to come and make some money, even though most people keep their valuables in the lockers, or if they're local, leave them at home. Anyway, there's always beach detectives at Bondi, especially on the weekend. That had to be the best job for a policeman: going to the beach, trying to look like any other beachgoer. They were always on the lookout for 'known criminals', and when they saw them up to no good, they'd grab them. It was strange to see a bloke in swimming trunks chase down a thief, then arrest them and march them off to the regular police.

Today though, this gang that came to the beach wasn't very smart. They were only teenagers, and the first thing they did when they turned up was start hiring all sorts of things on the beach – surf-o-planes, chairs, everything – but they paid with five- and ten-pound notes. Then they went up to the milk bars on Campbell Parade and started paying with big notes as well.

Everyone started reporting these teenagers who were throwing money around, and when they came back down to the beach, the police were waiting for them. As soon as they started picking things up, the police started chasing them. The thieves never stood a chance. They weren't used to running on sand, and soon got tired, while the beach detectives did it all the time.

It turned out this gang had been robbing beachgoers at Coogee and thought they'd avoid suspicion if they spent their money at a different beach. The police only recovered half the money because they'd already spent the other half before they got caught.

Sunday, 23 January 1938

'You awake, Nipper? C'mon. They're bitin'.'

Grampa Jack. Four-thirty this morning. Up I got, padded out of the house, squeezed the front door softly shut, then down to the rocks where the dinghy was waiting. Out in the water, so were the bream. Caught a couple of beauties with some beach worms Grampa Jack had picked up, just as the daylight started coming. That's often the way.

We could have caught a couple of swimmers too. There we were, out really early, out behind the shore break, which was pretty small, and these people came swimming past, doing laps of the beach. They didn't mind that there might be sharks. They dived in off the rocks at one end as soon as it was light enough to see, and they swam to the rocks at the other end, half a mile, easy, then they swam back. The people who did that were mostly men, but there were some women too. They weren't like the Icebergs, who swam all year round at their pool on the south end of the beach. The lap swimmers only swam in summer. Some did a couple of laps, others did a dozen or more.

Grampa Jack joked that he didn't know what kind of

bait the swimmers would go for but they were probably bad eating anyway. I didn't say anything to Grampa Jack about being well on my way to becoming one of them, except I go in from the beach then swim just outside the breakers.

Monday, 24 January 1938

The beach was really strange today. There was a really high tide and rough water and the sea cut away part of the beach. It took away all the sand, and there was clay underneath. The clay started dissolving and before you knew it, the whole bay had changed colour. Instead of blue it was a kind of yellowy grey. Grampa Jack reckoned it was the clay. He said there's lots of clay around Bondi, which they used to make bricks. There are a couple of brick-making places in Bondi that are digging up clay still. He pointed to some houses and said, 'See how they're the same colour as the sea? That's the colour of the clay the bricks are made from.' So the sea managed to find the clay and it turned the water grey.

There was nothing wrong with the water, and the waves were just the same, but no one wanted to swim in it. Who wants to swim in water the colour of bricks?

Tuesday, 25 January 1938

The water changed colour again today. It started changing at high tide, when the water came right up the beach. You couldn't see where the clay was but when the tide came up you could see all this coloured water coming up through the sand. Like, oozing up and turning the water a dirty colour, slowly filling the bay.

Wednesday, 26 January 1938

Happy Sesquicentenary!! Australia has turned a hundred and fifty years old. That is, unless you're Arthur, whose people have been here forever. Nevertheless, there were big celebrations today, especially on Sydney Harbour, where the festivities started with a re-enactment of the First Fleet landing. There was a huge parade through the city led by the mounted police and four trumpeters dressed as knights in shining armour. Then came the floats, over a hundred of them. The first showed the first Australians, the Aborigines, then came the Explorers, the Discovery of Gold, all the states, then various industries. Jamie would have liked the one for Dairying, which had a giant cow, Melba XV, the record holder for producing the most butterfat. They reckoned there were a million spectators for the parade, which is nearly everyone in Sydney, and I reckon it must have been true. There were people everywhere and it took ages to get home. We had to walk miles before we could get a tram. And today was just the beginning of the celebrations. They're supposed to go on until Anzac Day in April, including a huge surf carnival at Bondi in just a few weeks' time.

I managed to get a great souvenir, a poster showing a lifesaver standing over a surf reel looking out to sea. Behind him is the outline of Governor Phillip, on the bridge of his ship, in almost exactly the same position, except the lifesaver has much broader shoulders and would be taller if he was standing upright. It says, *150th Anniversary Celebrations of the Founding of AUSTRALIA*. I'm going to put it up over my bed in the sleepout.

Back at the beach, the water was back to normal. That's a good thing, because heaps of people who went to see the parade must have decided to round off their day with a swim at Bondi. There were tens of thousands of people on the sand or in the water, cooling off.

It was quite a day.

Saturday, 29 January 1938

Hey diary. Really big surf today. Quite a few rescues, but mostly the lifesavers were keeping people in the shallower water so they wouldn't get into trouble. One person, though, wasn't so lucky. He had a surf-o-plane, got out of his depth, and before he knew it he was in among the big waves. He couldn't touch bottom so he could push off and get back to shore. This young lifesaver named Mel, only about eighteen, went in with the belt and line. The waves looked pretty big from the shore, but when this young bloke got out there, he was just a tiny dot in among all this white foam, all on his own. The waves breaking over him were huge but he just kept going, under these huge breakers, up on the other side, out to this bloke who's still hanging on to his surf-o-plane.

The waves were so bad that the lifesavers got another reel ready with another belt and line in case Mel's line broke and he needed rescuing too. But the young fella just kept swimming out between these enormous breakers until he got to the chap in trouble. He made the bloke let go of the surf-o-plane then up went his arm to signal he's ready to be pulled in. The reelmen were extra careful, in case they wound too hard.

Most of the way, Mel had to swim with the bloke he'd rescued. The waves didn't so much break over them as just swallow them in boiling foam. But Mel just kept going. Swimming, disappearing into the waves, back out again.

Tell you what, when he got back into his depth, he could barely stand. Other lifesavers had to bring the bloke he saved in to the shore. A couple helped Mel. Afterwards he just sat on the shore, trying to catch his breath. It took him quite a while.

Grampa Jack reckons it was the rescue of the summer. It was too rough to take the surf boat out, at least not Bondi's rickety old thing, so Mel had to go out alone. Another thing Grampa Jack told me is that Mel comes from way out in western Sydney every day to be a lifesaver.

'He's not a weekender,' Grampa Jack said, 'so he catches a train from Merrylands, where he lives, to Central, then a tram to Bondi. Takes him two hours in the morning, two hours at night. Saturday and Sunday. Just to be a lifesaver.'

Sunday, 30 January 1938

It's the saddest night of the year. The summer holidays are over and school starts tomorrow. Year Seven at Bondi Primary. I could go to Sydney High, but it's easier to walk down the road than it is to catch a couple of trams. Same for Rachel and Damo.

Today the beach was almost as packed as a Bondi tram! People getting in all the holidays they can, especially with the sesquicentenary bringing so many to Sydney for the celebrations. The lifesavers were busy all day today, just with so many people, and Grampa Jack was relieved when the second patrol ended and people started leaving. The promenade this evening was really special too. At least for all the kids, who knew that the days of sun, sand, swimming and freedom were over. For the shark fishermen it was just another Sunday, and they caught a few big ones, even with the shark net being used all summer.

Funny thing, the shark net people claim they were successful because no one was taken by a shark all summer. True, but no one at Bondi had been taken by a shark for nearly ten years before that, without the net.

I've kind of decided that I'll stay at school at least

until I'm old enough to become a beach inspector or join the army. Well, actually, Mum and Dad helped me decide. Meanwhile, Josie put on a bit of a cry tonight. Miserable that summer is over and school is starting again. And she likes school! Me, I just hope my new teacher isn't as bad as Mrs Kearsley. If he or she is, nothing will make me stay. Not even Mum and Dad.

Monday, 31 January 1938

Well, that could have been worse. Mr Hester, my new teacher, is really nice. Even though he said, 'Ah yes, young McCutcheon. Mrs Kearsley has told me all about you.' He's an older chap, been in the war like Grampa Jack, and he has a wooden leg. He's very strict – sit up straight, no talking – but he's also funny, and he knows lots of poetry. Sometimes, while we were working on an exercise, he'd just stand by the window reciting things, like *Gunga Din*:

> *Tho' I've belted you and flayed you,*
> *By the livin' Gawd that made you,*
> *You're a better man than I am, Gunga Din!*

I wondered if he meant that about us. He's a big fan of Rudyard Kipling. And Blake:

Tiger, tiger, burning bright,
In the forests of the night,
What immortal hand or eye,
Could frame thy fearful symmetry?

He told us about what we were going to learn this year and that if anyone was having trouble understanding anything, to let him know and he'd try to help them. He told us that he knew some kids might be leaving as soon as they were old enough but in the meantime he wanted to give them as much knowledge as he could to get them ahead in the big, wide world. He said, 'The more you know, the more successful you'll be.'

I'd never heard anyone put it that way but it made a lot of sense. Even being a lifesaver was like that. The more you know, like Grampa Jack, the better you'll be.

Wednesday, 2 February 1938

It's amazing. I'm really liking school. Rachel, Damo and

me are all in the one class, which is a lot smaller than last year's. And all the kids we hang around with at Bondi, or a lot of them, we're together all the time. Mr Hester is like the leader of the gang. He's always saying things like, 'Now, here's something that will challenge your young minds.' And it does. It'd be great if school was always like this. But I guess even school has to end sometime. Then the big, wide world.

The waves today were big curlers coming in from far away, in long steady lines, one after the other. Must be a big storm somewhere way out to sea. I went for my usual swim first thing this morning but decided not to swim a length. I had to go a long way out just to get past the breakers. I realised that if I got into trouble, it was a long way back to the beach. So instead I went out and back about half a dozen times, which was probably longer. I reckon it was a hundred yards each way and it was harder as I swam out through the breakers. It felt harder anyway.

Saturday, 5 February 1938

The beach was really rough today. Big surf, like it's been for the last few days. Too rough to go for my ocean swim.

Even just going out and back a couple of times left me too tired to go again. All through the day, a lot of people needed rescuing. In the middle of the afternoon, as the tide was falling, the sea would go quiet for a while, then these big waves would come, almost out of nowhere, and as people had ventured further out when it was quiet, they'd get caught by the big waves. There was a sand bank, with a deep channel behind, and people suddenly found themselves pulled off the bank by the backwash from the wave. The lifesavers in the middle of the beach did seventy rescues during the afternoon patrol. Seventy. That's a rescue every five minutes of their five-hour patrol. Sometimes it was more often than that. Little wonder they were pretty tired by the end of the day.

Black Sunday, 6 February 1938

Hey diary. It's late at night. I've woken up after a long sleep but I have to write this down. It's been a terrible, terrible day. Down at Bondi this afternoon, four people, maybe five, have been drowned. And it could have been a lot more. And one of them could have been me.

This is what happened. The waves were just like

yesterday, really big, rough surf, but the head beach inspector who was in charge this afternoon hadn't been on patrol on Saturday, and hadn't seen how many rescues there'd been. In the morning the other lifesavers had moved everyone to the north end of the beach where the waves weren't so big, but after lunch he decided to put flags in the middle of the beach as well. It wasn't long before people started getting into trouble. And then, well, I've never seen anything like it.

About half-past two, a lot of the Bondi Surf Club members who weren't on patrol started gathering to practise for the anniversary surf carnival that's on in a couple of weeks. There must have been about seventy or eighty of them down on the sand as well as the normal patrol. It was pure luck that they were there.

Out in the water, there were all these people on the bank in the middle of the beach. Everything seemed pretty normal, just another sunny afternoon at Bondi. Then there was one of those long lulls in the waves, like there'd been yesterday. Sometimes the ocean just seems to take a moment to catch its breath, but anyone who knows reckons it's just gathering itself for something big.

All these people went a bit further out on the bank

to catch these smaller waves that were coming. Lots of them had surf-o-planes, and they were lured out into water that was only waist deep so they could push off the bottom and catch a wave. Lots of them couldn't swim but they must have thought that if they didn't go out of their depth and had a surf-o-plane, they'd be right.

Unfortunately, today was different. You could see these three big waves – they always come in threes – rolling towards the beach from a long, long way out. If there'd been only one, it might have been all right. As they got closer to shore they just got bigger and bigger until they were giants. As the first one came, most of the people on the bank didn't think about trying to catch it. They were struggling through the water to get away. They looked so tiny in front of this rising wall of water. Lots got caught under it when it broke and lost their surf-o-planes as the boiling surf and turbulence tumbled them over and over. When they came to the surface, the water was suddenly much deeper. But they only had a few seconds before the second wave broke over them. Most of the surf-o-planes that hadn't been swept away by the first wave were ripped from their struggling owners by the second. By now, all the people who couldn't swim were panicking.

As the third wave rose higher and higher, there was no longer anyone standing in front of it. All you could see were the heads of those who could still swim and lots of desperate people thrashing in the water. As the last wave toppled over and broke in a terrible roar, the only other thing you could hear was people screaming just before the foam engulfed them.

The third wave rolled over the struggling swimmers and ran seething to the shore. It pushed so far up the beach that it reached a lot of people who were sitting on their towels. In the sea, the water was much higher than it had been, and people desperately sought to touch the sandy bottom that was there just moments before. Hundreds were struggling to stay afloat, splashing desperately and crying out in the water.

Then it got worse. Everyone who knows the surf knows that all the water that had come in on those three great waves had to go back out. Everyone on the beach could only watch in horror as this mass of terrified people, hundreds and hundreds of them, were dragged out into deeper water.

There was panic everywhere. Desperate people were clinging to anything or anyone that would keep them afloat. People on the shore were screaming to their friends and family that they could see were in trouble. Everyone who could reach the shore was streaming out of the water. There was terror in their eyes. But all around them, others were racing into the water.

Lifesavers.

They'd all seen what happened. While the regular patrol manned the belts and reels on that section of the beach, many of the other lifesavers just ran, and I mean *ran*, straight into the surf. Others were running to the nearest reels along the beach and in fours carried them back to bring into action. From both ends of the beach other lifesavers came racing down the sand to help in the rescue. Some grabbed a belt and line if there was one available, others just ran along the beach until they were close enough to all the people in trouble and then dived straight into the water, into the middle of the chaos.

Out in the surf men were grabbing at the lifesavers who came near, people were being dragged under, some were waving their arms feebly, hoping someone would come to them. As a lifesaver brought a person to shore, crowds pressed in to see if it was their loved one. Often they were limp, as though they were dead, and the lifesavers handed them over to care then turned round and ran straight back into the water.

People tried to help the men on the reels so more lifesavers could go into the water but they kept winding the reels too fast, especially when the water from a wave was sucking the lifesaver back out, and they actually made things worse by causing the lines to snap.

Amid the pandemonium, I noticed a woman not far from the shore. She was out of the deepest water but she couldn't make any ground to get back to the sand bank. As each wave came in, she was driven under, came struggling to the surface and was then sucked back out. She was trying to stand or to swim but she didn't seem to have the strength. I looked around to see if someone could help her, but there was no one but us kids.

'There's a lady in trouble, just there,' I said, but no one could see where I was pointing.

Another wave came in and she went under again. It seemed to take forever for her to come back up. Her head was barely above water.

'There!' I shouted. I couldn't understand why no one else could see her.

I started walking towards the water. I can remember

someone saying, 'Nipper, what are you doing?'

Then I didn't hear anything because I'd started running. If I didn't do something, the woman was going to drown. I couldn't just stand there. Then I was jumping the waves in the shore break and running through the shallows into the deeper water. Down at the shore you could see the size of the waves breaking on the back of the bank. Huge waves. But I could still see the woman, barely struggling now. I dived under a wave, came up, couldn't touch bottom, and started swimming. Under another wave.

As I felt the water sucking me towards the next wave, I started having doubts. I thought about turning back. The current was strong. Really strong. Then I saw the woman, almost sinking. Not so far now. But still further out. I was getting really scared.

Thinking I shouldn't have done this.

I wanted to turn back. Out there, all around me, you could really see how desperate the people were. They were grabbing at lifesavers, surf-o-planes, anything to help them float. I could see lifesavers pushing some people away and struggling to help others who were unconscious. Then I was close to the woman. She'd given up. I could actually see it. She had no fight left.

I really don't know how I did it but I made myself put my head down, kick hard and keep swimming out to her. It was a bit like all those times I've had to push myself to swim a bit further to do a length of the beach. Don't give up. Just a bit more. Under a wave. Up. And there she was.

'I've got you, missus,' I said. 'I've got you.'

She didn't say anything. She barely moved. Her hair was strewn all over her face but she made no effort to push it away. I knew from what Grampa Jack said that you have to be careful of people who are drowning. They'll grab you and force you under, so they can stay afloat. You have to get behind them, support their head with one hand, and swim with the other. But this lady didn't grab. She was too weak to do anything.

'Just try to float,' I said, as I got behind her, arm around her torso, hand under her chin, just like us kids had done to each other, pretending to be lifesavers, hundreds of times. 'When a wave comes, deep breath, like now!'

I don't know if she took a breath or didn't, but I still had her when we came back up. It had taken most of

173

my strength to do it. I started kicking and swimming to the shore but we'd only got about a couple of feet before the next wave hit. And the next and the next. By then I'd found the only way I could hang on for the waves was to wrap both arms around her. Then when the wave passed, kick hard to get to the surface, then swim a bit.

I wasn't sure we were getting anywhere. I turned my head for a moment. There was the beach, good old Bondi, but it seemed so terribly far away.

I kicked and swam, kicked and swam. Another wave. We were thrown and tumbled. I hung on, kicked back to the surface. Kicked and swam.

'Don't worry, missus,' I said. 'I won't let you go.'

I don't know whether she heard or not but I think I was really talking to myself. I was so tired I didn't know how much longer I could keep a grip on her and keep swimming, but I was determined to keep going as long as I could. Maybe someone would help us. Another wave, back up. And then … I felt something brush my foot. Sand!

We'd reached the bank. I could have cried, I was so happy.

Keep kicking, Nipper, keep swimming, I told myself.

Just a little further. At last I could push off the bottom, push closer to shore, into shallower water.

'We're on the bank!' I shouted. 'We've made it!'

Except we hadn't. The woman was too weak to stand up. So I ended up holding her and trying to drag her. She was too heavy. And the current on the bank kept trying to pull her back out. I found I could keep hold of her and stop her being sucked out but I couldn't drag her any further as the sea tried to take her back into the depths.

I didn't know that Rachel, Damo and Josie were watching the whole thing. They managed to get some grownups to come out to us. When this man and woman appeared beside me and took hold of the woman, I couldn't believe it. Between us we got her into the shallows and then there were people everywhere. Hands lifting and carrying the woman to the shore. Someone tried to lift me, thinking I was being saved, but I shook them off.

We got her to the shore, where she slumped on the ground, sitting with her head down between her knees. She was shivering terribly and I heard someone shouting for blankets. I knelt beside her and said, 'You're safe now, missus. You'll be all right.'

She slowly lifted her head, her wet hair all around her face. At first I didn't recognise her. Then I realised who she was.

'Mrs Kearsley!'

Monday, 7 February 1938

That's right, diary. I saved my teacher from last year. The one who, well, you know. So you can't imagine what school was like today. But I'll get to that. I was too tired to write any more last night, so I'll continue on where I left off.

So there's Mrs Kearsley and me on the beach, looking at each other. And it's like, of all the people, on all the beaches, in all the world, why did it have to be you? Just for a moment, I reckon we both thought it.

Mrs Kearsley dropped her eyes and took my hand.

'Thank you, Nipper.'

She thanked me. For saving her life. I can't begin to describe what that made me feel like.

Then Damo and Rachel got back with a blanket and we wrapped Mrs Kearsley up tight. At some point a doctor ran up and quickly checked her over and said,

'Look after her. Call for assistance if she has a turn.'

So we stayed with her until she started to come good.

All around us the scene was unlike anything I'd ever seen on Bondi. There were people with arms linked holding the crowds of people back, while on the sand, bodies were lined up with lifesavers and doctors trying to resuscitate them. People were running from place to place, frantically searching for people who were missing. Some people were crying from the distress of what had happened, others were slumped on the beach exhausted by their desperate effort to survive.

By then, nearly everyone had left the water, right along the beach. There were still lifesavers out though, swimming back and forth looking for anyone who might have gone under and was drowning beneath the waves. The usually happy Sunday afternoon on the beach had been replaced by tragedy.

Mrs Kearsley was really struggling to get her strength back, so she asked us to help her home. We found her things, then walked a little bit, then rested, then walked a bit more, until we got to her flat, a couple of blocks back from the beach. Thank goodness it was the ground floor. I don't think she'd have got up the stairs.

As it was, she collapsed into a chair, and we got blankets and wrapped her up warm, even though it wasn't a cold day. Then we offered her a cup of tea.

'Not too hot,' I suggested, 'With lots of sugar.'

That's what Grampa Jack reckoned was best for someone who'd nearly drowned.

'Sounds wonderful,' Mrs Kearsley said.

We put the kettle on to boil, then sort of waited around, not knowing what else to do.

It was while we were standing there that I noticed a photograph in the middle of Mrs Kearsley's mantelpiece. It was a picture of a young woman and a young soldier. I went over and looked closer. The woman in the photograph was Mrs Kearsley, but when she was much younger. I went to pick the photo up but she stopped me.

'David,' she said, 'please be careful. That's all I have left of my husband.'

'What happened to him?' It was a bit rude to blurt out such a question but as far as I knew, there'd never been a Mr Kearsley.

'My Reginald went missing in action in 1916.'

Suddenly I felt awful. 'And I called you a ...'

She held up a hand. 'You weren't to know.'

Damo and Rachel made the tea while I sat with Mrs Kearsley.

'We were married a week before his embarkation,' she said. 'He's never grown old and I've never stopped loving him.'

I felt terrible. Kicked myself all the way home.

By the time I got there, everyone was talking about what had happened at the beach. It turned out that many, many people had been pulled from the water unconscious. Almost all of them were revived but, sadly, four didn't make it.

It was a strange feeling. There was a sense of tragedy at the loss of life, but also a realisation that if it hadn't been for the courage of the lifesavers, the disaster could have been far worse. Later in the day, a check was done of all the lockers in the Pavilion. One still contained someone's belongings. The police were trying to find whose they were, but it was feared that someone else had drowned and their body was still in the water.

Thanks to Josie, Mum and Dad knew what had happened with Mrs Kearsley, but they seemed more worried about me. Mum kept saying, 'Thank God you're safe.'

Grampa Jack came in later. He'd been down on

the beach. He'd saved a couple of people and helped resuscitate several more, but he'd heard about me. By then I was lying down, really tired, but he walked straight into the sleepout, and well, I've never seen him so angry.

'You stupid, stupid boy!' he shouted at me. 'You could have been killed!' This while he was picking me up in his arms and was squeezing me so hard I could barely breathe. Then he sort of tossed me on the bed like a rag doll and grabbed me by the shoulders and pulled my face close to his and said, 'Promise me, Nipper. Promise me you will never do anything so foolish again.'

I was pretty shocked. I'd never seen Grampa Jack like this and it really scared me, but I simply couldn't do what he wanted me to. 'I'm sorry, Grampa Jack,' I said. 'I know I'm not a lifesaver but I couldn't just stand there and watch someone die.'

For a moment I thought Grampa Jack was going to explode. His face went incredibly red. Then he tried to say something but the only thing that came out was a strange little squeak. And then he rushed out of the sleepout.

There was long silence, then I heard Grampa Jack telling Mum and Dad more about what had happened on the beach.

He reckoned two hundred and fifty people had suddenly been swept into deep water. Most of them couldn't swim, and almost all needed rescuing. The lifesavers' motto might be 'ready, aye ready' but not even Bondi's lifesavers were ready to rescue that many people at one time. They were only about seventy or eighty yards from the shore but many were clawing and grabbing at anything floating or anyone near in incredible panic. This while lifesavers were trying to get them back to safety.

Because a lot of members of the lifesaving club had come down on the beach to practise for the surf carnival, seventy or eighty of them, it was sheer good fortune that nearly a hundred lifesavers were on hand for the mass rescue of so many people. Mr McDonald and his family, who ran the surf-o-plane hire, ran down with dozens of them to help get anything people could use to stay afloat out into the water. Lifesavers swam out with them, saved someone, then left the float so others could use it to help keep their heads above water.

There was almost as much distress on the beach as there was in the water. People became increasingly frantic as they looked for missing friends or relatives but worse still, some tried to help loved ones who were brought from the water unconscious, interfering with the efforts of lifesavers to revive them. They were pulling lifesavers away from bodies, trying to see if the person being saved was someone they knew.

Before he went home, Grampa Jack came back into the sleepout, where I was up, writing in you, diary.

'There's one other thing, Nipper,' he said, giving me a huge hug. 'If they gave bronze medallions to twelve-year-olds, you just earned yours today.'

So this morning, I really wondered what it would be like going to school. I expected the entire sixth class would hate me for saving their teacher. I couldn't have been more wrong. They had a special assembly where the headmaster explained that Mrs Kearsley had been involved in what the newspapers were calling Black Sunday and was still recovering. Then the headmaster called me up to the stage.

'And this is the hero of the hour,' he said. 'David McCutcheon dived into the surf and, at great risk to himself, brought Mrs Kearsley to safety. I want to take this opportunity to express the profound gratitude of the whole school, its pupils, parents and staff. In his brave deed, David has shown himself to be the embodiment of the best qualities of Bondi Public School and Bondi's finest, our surf lifesavers. I ask you to join me in giving him three rousing cheers.'

And the whole school did just that while I blushed as red as it's possible to blush. Then all the teachers shook my hand or kissed me on the cheek. It was a relief to get to class, although even there, Mr Hester couldn't resist making a fuss. Before class started he had me stand up and told everyone they should be proud of what I'd done. Rachel and Damo poked me and smiled and said, 'We are, we all are'.

Then Mr Hester recited the last bit of *Gunga Din,* except he changed the name:

Though I've belted you and flayed you,
By the livin' Gawd that made you,
You're a better man than I am, Mr McCutcheon.

He hasn't actually belted or flayed me. Then at little lunch everyone wanted to know all about what had happened. At lunchtime they all wanted to hear the story again. Even some of the teachers lingered nearby to hear what I was saying. Walking home from school,

Josie wanted to hold my hand the whole way.

'So everyone knows you're my big brother,' she said.

Then Mr Smith wanted to know all about it, even though I had a lot of groceries to deliver, so by the time I met Grampa Jack to walk home from the Diggers, I was sick of talking about what had happened. Anyway, Grampa Jack knew most of it. Actually, we didn't talk much at all on the way home. Just went to look at the water like we always do. The waves today wouldn't have hurt a fly. Nothing like it had been on the weekend.

Tuesday, 8 February 1938

Mrs Kearsley came to school today. It was a bit awkward when I first saw her. Everyone was watching us, expecting something special to happen. I didn't know quite what to do or say, and I don't think she knew either. But we walked towards each other anyway.

'Good morning, David,' she said.

'Good morning, Mrs Kearsley,' I answered. 'I hope you're feeling better.'

'Much, thank you,' she said.

'I'm glad,' I said.

Everyone was listening. How could I say how relieved

I was that nothing bad had happened to either of us?

She put her hand out to shake mine, and I took it. Then she said, 'I'll never forget what you did.'

We shook hands and I said, 'I've already put it in my diary.'

Mrs Kearsley looked surprised for a moment and then she smiled. 'I know better than to ask you to show it to me.'

There was more in the newspapers today about what happened on 'Black Sunday'. They described the scene on the beach as being like a battlefield. It was estimated that sixty people were brought from the water unconscious, and forty of them weren't able to be immediately revived.

The police had put out a call on public radio asking all doctors and ambulance men who might be near the beach to go there at once to assist. People came from everywhere to help.

The people who died were all men: Bernard F. Byrne, Ronald D. McGregor, Charles L. Sauer (aka Sweety) and Leslie R. Potter. The man reported missing is Michael Kennedy (aka Taylor), from Surry Hills. The police went to his home and had to break the news to his wife.

One newspaper reported that what was remarkable

out in the water was that most of the panic was with the men. The women who were in trouble were much more calm. According to one lifesaver who was interviewed: 'The men were crying like girls, shrieking with terror and shouting wildly for help. On the other hand, the girls were calm and seemed to wait quietly, keeping above water as best they could until they were rescued.'

There was quite a bit of pride in what an American doctor, Marshall Dyer, who had helped save many lives, had to say: 'I have never seen, nor expect to see again, such a magnificent achievement. It was a scene I'll never forget, and when I get back to the States I'll tell them about your surf men. There are none like them in the world.'

Wednesday, 9 February 1938

Hey diary. This is an easy entry to write. I'm not sure if it's cheating not to write your diary yourself but I wanted to glue in this newspaper article about what happened on Sunday.

BONDI SURF TRAGEDY.

Ena Stockley

Many Acts of Bravery.

So many brave actions were performed at Bondi on Sunday, 6 February, when 200 surfers were swept out to sea that Sergeant Gorman, of the Bondi police, has found it impossible to single out any individual rescuers for special commendation.

In a report to the Deputy Commissioner of Police, Mr T. J. Lynch, Sergeant Gorman said that 80 members of the Bondi Lifesaving Club either swam out to surfers in difficulties, or assisted in the work of resuscitating men and women brought ashore. Eight life lines were used, but many life savers went a long distance out to bring in swimmers.

It had been reported to the police that Miss E. Stockley, a former champion swimmer, had risked her life saving others from the fierce undertow. Sergeant Gorman said that he had interviewed Miss Stockley, who said that she had helped to bring many ashore, but not risked her life.

Sergeant Gorman mentioned Dr. Marshall Dyer, of the United States, who, he said, worked for more than two hours helping to resuscitate rescued surfers, and who remained on the beach until all had recovered. He also referred to the

services rendered by six officers from the Eastern Suburbs
Ambulance with three ambulance wagons, and to the help
given by Drs. Ping, Hardie, and McKellar, all of Bondi, in
reviving many unconscious persons.

"It is impossible to single out any Individuals for
special commendation," added Sergeant Gorman. "This
view is also shared by the officials of the Bondi Lifesaving
Club, but there is no doubt that the work performed by the
members of the club and others prevented a more serious
catastrophe."

Impossible to single out individuals? That's easy for
the newspaper to say. They're not going to Bondi Public.
Everyone's treating me like I'm a hero, and I'm starting to
wish they'd treat me like normal. The only person I don't
mind treating me different is Mrs Kearsley. We haven't
really talked about what happened, but whenever I see
her, it makes me feel just a bit, I dunno, but it's good. Plus
she isn't mean to me any more, so that's good too.

Thursday, 10 February 1938

The missing man's body washed up on the beach this

afternoon. Grampa Jack told me when I went down to the Diggers to walk him home.

As usual we went the long way home along the promenade, looking at the beach. We didn't talk much until we were on our own. We just stopped and looked at the sea for a while.

It was our beach, the place we spent all our lives, and it had just killed five people. Five. The lifesavers had done everything they could, but it still hadn't been enough. Grampa Jack must have been thinking the same thing.

'It could have been a lot worse,' he said. 'Imagine if it had been a week earlier, before school holidays finished.'

Grampa Jack was right. If people were still on holidays, people from all over coming to the beach with their kids, there could have been thousands more on the beach and in the water. The lifesavers might have been overwhelmed.

Then he said, 'So, young lifesaver. How does it feel to be a hero?'

'Grampa Jack,' I said. 'I don't think I like it.'

Grampa Jack nodded. 'What you did was very brave.'

We watched a couple of seagulls argue over who got to stand on which bit of sand. Then I said, 'I never felt brave. The whole time I was scared nearly to death.'

Grampa Jack gave a little chuckle. 'So now you know,' he said. He gave me a pat on the shoulder. 'Come on, young lifesaver. Don't want to miss your dinner.'

It's only now, while I'm writing this, that I noticed Grampa Jack called me a lifesaver, twice.

Saturday, 12 February 1938

I went back to the beach today. Up early with Rachel and Damo and Josie, and we went down together. Normally we just chuck our stuff on the sand and dive in the water, but instead I sat on my towel and looked at it. Nice bank there, good even break, bit of a rip on the left. No worries, especially if you swam between the flags.

It all looked so normal.

'Last one in's a rotten egg,' Josie said, and tore off down the beach.

My little sister wasn't worried about the surf. She was never scared of anything.

'You comin', Nipper?' Damo said. 'Rachel might need savin'.'

I went in and for a while I didn't like it. Everyone

else was having fun but not me.

'Come on, Nipper,' Rachel shouted as she zipped past on her surf-o-plane. 'Get your hair wet.'

She came back out to where I was standing waist-deep. 'Do you want a go?'

She pushed her surf-o-plane at me.

'Nah,' I said, 'I'm right.'

She splashed me with water. I splashed her back and then she took off.

I felt really strange.

Then I saw a slightly bigger wave coming. It was either dive under or get knocked backwards. I took a deep breath and dived. As soon as my head went under, everything changed. There was that little burst of pressure as the wave passed over me. I kicked and swam and I was blowing out air as I hit the surface. When I came up, I was smiling.

It was still the same ocean. Except maybe I had a little more respect for it. No, not maybe. Definitely. As for it being dangerous, when I looked back at the beach, there was the lifesaving patrol.

Ready, aye ready.

Sunday, 13 February 1938

What is going on? As if Black Sunday wasn't bad enough, today there was a worse tragedy on Sydney Harbour. A ferry has capsized and they think as many as twenty people may have drowned. What happened was, there were a lot of people out on the harbour to farewell the American navy cruiser, USS *Louisville*, which was on a goodwill trip ('Showing the Germans that Australia has some powerful friends,' Dad said) and this ferry had gone out with a large number of passengers to enjoy the sight. However, the ferry was overloaded and tipped right over, and then it sank. It all happened in less than a minute, and hundreds of people ended up in the water. The *Louisville* and all the other vessels in the area immediately went to the rescue but people are saying that far more people have died than those who died on Black Sunday. It's a bit scary to go through one disaster on one weekend and have another one take place just a couple of miles away on the next weekend. Makes you wonder what's next.

Monday, 14 February 1938

The newspapers are full of what happened yesterday.

The ferry was called the *Rodney* and was thought to be carrying over two hundred people when it capsized. When it did, sixteen passengers drowned. The owner, and the *Rodney*'s captain, Charles Rosman, survived. There was a photo of the *Rodney* just before it tipped and it shows the ferry leaning right over, with lots of people crowded on the upper deck to get a better view. There were even some on top of the wheelhouse. You could see the vessel was already leaning over dangerously.

Grampa Jack and I knew that meant trouble. When we take the dinghy out on the sea we're always careful to keep in the middle of the boat so it won't tip and give a wave a chance to sink us.

The newspaper also said that a lot of the people who died were young women who had gone out on the ferry to wave goodbye to the sailors who'd won their hearts during the *Louisville*'s stay in Sydney. The Yanks, as people called them, were very popular. There were quite a few who had come down to Bondi on shore leave, and most of them had a girl on their arm.

Grampa Jack and I read the reports together and Grampa Jack said something interesting. He noticed that almost as many people fell into the water as were swept out at Bondi the week before. But the water on the harbour was calm while the surf at Bondi was rough. Despite that, the lifesavers had saved all but five people but the rescuers on the harbour hadn't been able to save sixteen.

'It's more dangerous in the surf,' he said, 'but with a patrol on standby, all of them trained to handle an emergency, you're actually safer.'

Still, the capsize shouldn't have happened. The newspaper said that the *Rodney* was only allowed to have sixty people on the upper deck. When it capsized, there were more than a hundred.

Tuesday, 15 February 1938

I went down for my early morning swim today. My first time on my own since Black Sunday. Did a length of the beach easy. Body surfed into the beach. Went back out. Swam back in. Nobody saw me doing it. It was just me and the waves again.

When I got home though, Dad already had some toast waiting for me. He didn't look up from his newspaper when I came in, not even when I said, 'Thanks, Dad.'

He just muttered, 'Ready, aye ready, Nip.'

He read his newspaper while I munched my toast.

Ready, aye ready, the motto of the Bondi Lifesaving Club. I asked Mum this afternoon what it really meant. She reckons the *aye* part is Scottish. It means yes, like when sailors say 'aye, aye, captain', but it can also mean always. So ready, aye ready means ready, yes ready or it means ready, always ready. Either way, that's what lifesavers are.

Thursday, 17 February 1938

I can't believe it. I had a run in with Mrs Kearsley! It was nothing really that set me off, but now I think she hates me. So here we go again. And it's not just Mrs Kearsley. And it's all my fault.

What happened is, at lunchtime, just trying to play cricket with me mates, they were insisting on making me captain of my team and letting me be Don Bradman without even arguing. And there's all these teachers smiling at me all the time. And Mrs Kearsley really didn't do anything. She called me David and I must have just had enough. Anyway, I lost my temper. Nothing new, I know, but I yelled at her.

'Me name's Nipper!'

The look on her face. It was like I'd slapped her.

Mr Hester heard me too. Well, half the school did. And didn't he let me have it.

'Of all the people in this school,' he bellowed, 'you should be leading by example, Mr McCutcheon.'

'Tough luck,' I shouted, and I stormed off.

That should have got me into more trouble but I heard Mrs Kearsley say, 'Mr Hester. Please, let him go.'

A bit later the bell went and we all moved into class. Mr Hester looked like he was going to explode, but he didn't say anything. I was just as angry.

I wasn't much better when I went to walk home with Grampa Jack. We got to the beach and were looking at the waves, all choppy from a nor-easter, and I was still in a bit of a mood.

'Something troubling you, young lifesaver?' Grampa Jack asked.

'I'm not a lifesaver!' I shouted, and I was almost crying. 'Why won't you just call me Nipper?'

I left him there. Ran off actually. Couldn't go home. Went up on to the heath up behind North Bondi. Walked along a bit. Kept going until I found that place old Arthur showed me. Where he reckons they turned boys into men. There were all these white pegs around it. So now someone was going to build there. I felt like pulling them all out. Wouldn't have done any good. Instead I just sat there on the edge of the rock for a while. Thinking. That didn't help much either. Sooner or later I'd have to go back and face the music.

Everyone had eaten dinner when I got home. There was a plate keeping warm in the oven.

Mum put my dinner on the table. Dad closed the doors to the dining room and he and Mum sat down beside me while I ate. I wouldn't be running out of there, that was for sure. They didn't say anything until I was finished and sat, staring at the table, waiting to be excused.

Then Dad said, 'Rough day?'

Not quite what I was expecting, so I thought for a moment. 'I'm sick of people being nice to me,' I mumbled.

I thought they'd laugh, but Mum just put her hand on Dad's. Even so, he couldn't help himself. 'Would it help if I threatened you with the washing up?'

Mum didn't scold. Instead she said, 'Darling, has it occurred to you that you might have earned their respect?'

'I don't care,' I wailed. 'Why can't they treat me like all the other kids?'

'Really,' Dad said. 'I thought you couldn't wait to grow up and be a lifesaver.'

'You know that?'

He gave me one of his serious businesslike looks. 'The swimming every other morning. The big poster over your bed,' he said. 'Bit of a giveaway.'

'Anyway,' I said. 'After what I just did, I doubt anyone will respect me any more.'

'I think you'll find they're a bit more understanding,' Mum said.

'Give them time, Nipper,' Dad said. 'They'll settle down. Meanwhile, do you need any help sorting things out with all the people you've upset?'

Apparently I wasn't in trouble. Well, I was, but not with them.

'Thanks, Dad, I'll be right,' I said. 'To begin with, I'm sorry I came home late.'

Anyway, better finish up and go to bed. It's late and I'm tired, although I'm not sure I'll get much sleep. Out in the kitchen I can hear Dad grumbling, 'Senior economist, major bank, and here I am, stuck doing the dishes.'

Friday, 18 February 1938

It's all good. This morning I got up and had breakfast early, asked Josie to walk to school with Rachel and Damo because I had things to do, and headed off early. Mum and Dad noticed but didn't say anything. They just let me go.

I went around to Grampa Jack's and found him rummaging about in his backyard.

'Nipper,' he said, instead of 'young lifesaver'. But he did say, 'Good morning to you, young man.'

'Hi, Grampa Jack,' I said. 'I've come to apologise for yesterday.'

'No need, Nip,' he said, much to my surprise. 'You were right.'

'I was?'

'Yeah, mate,' he answered. 'I was so proud of you, I got a bit carried away. I didn't notice it was all a bit too much.'

'Thanks, Grampa Jack,' I said, 'but I shouldn't have treated you like that.'

'I know,' he said, 'but I understand. *Nipper* it is then. But I'm givin' you fair warning. When you get your bronze medallion and become a real lifesaver, brace yourself, because I'm not going to hide how proud I'll be.'

It was the same over at Mrs Kearsley's. She accepted my apology and admitted things had been a bit strange. Anyway, we came to a little understanding. She'll still call me David at school, you know, for appearances, but she'll definitely call me Nipper if she sees me anywhere else. So that's good.

I think she must have spoken to Mr Hester as well. He hasn't been paying me as much attention, although he did recite *Gunga Din* again. He changed the name at the end back to Gunga Din, but he was looking straight at me when he said it.

Saturday, 19 February 1938

A great day for the Sesquicentenary Surf Carnival and for Bondi. It hardly seems real that only two weeks ago there was a disaster at the beach. And last week a disaster on the harbour. Today couldn't have been more different. Half of Sydney must have turned up for the biggest surf carnival in the country. There were clubs from every state and from New Zealand. There was even an English lord.

The march past was the most spectacular I've ever

seen. More than thirty clubs competed and they were so good that six teams tied for first, including North Bondi. So they had a march off and North Bondi won! Plus Bondi won the rescue and resuscitation race, which got a huge cheer from the crowd. North Bondi also won the junior surf boat, but Bondi didn't do so well in our ratty old tub. The star though, once again, was Bob Newbiggin from Newcastle, who only got his bronze medallion at Christmas. He won the junior belt race and the junior championship. I'd give anything to be half as good as him.

Mum and Dad were very pleased with themselves too. They'd spent the day fundraising with all the other club supporters and they reckoned they made heaps of money. Mum reckons Black Sunday has made people realise how important lifesavers are in making the beach safe.

'They were really digging deep,' she said.

Dad reckons that if things keep going like they are, the club will soon be able to afford a new surf boat. That would give our senior crew a real boost in competitions, not to mention doing rescues.

The only person who wasn't so happy about the day was Rachel. We were helping pack up when she started complaining.

'These lifesavers. They are all men,' she said. 'Why can't girls be lifesavers too?'

'I dunno,' Damo said. 'That's the rules. Maybe women aren't strong enough.'

'This woman, Ena Stockley, on Black Sunday,' Rachel pointed out, 'in the newspaper it said she saved many lives. She was strong enough.'

'But she's a champion swimmer,' I said. 'Besides, you want the lifesavers rescuing people, not distracted by pretty girls.'

Rachel still wanted to argue, while Damo and I reckoned things were right the way they were. Then Grampa Jack chipped in. 'Rachel's right. It doesn't matter who you are. If you're good enough, you're good enough. And don't forget, it may be the lifesavers who do all the hero stuff but it's people like your mum, Nipper, who help with all the organising, fundraising, even cooking lamingtons. We'd be stuffed without 'em.'

'I can do more than cook lamingtons,' Rachel said, and no one argued with that.

Sunday, 20 February 1938

'Nipper. C'mon, they're bitin.' Grampa Jack was tapping at my window this morning. Apparently the surf carnival hadn't tired him out.

We launched the dinghy and rowed out, baited up and sat for a while, just getting nibbles. The light was growing and Grampa Jack and I were back to being mates, so that was all right.

Then Grampa Jack asked, 'Hey Nip, has Mrs Kearsley been back to the beach?'

I said, 'I dunno.'

Grampa Jack nodded. 'Reckon she might be a bit shy of the waves now?'

'Yeah,' I said, 'I would be, after what happened.'

I was sure of that because I had been too.

Then Grampa Jack said, 'Maybe she'd come down if you asked her. If you bring her, we'll make sure she's all right.'

So this morning, I went round to her flat and asked her if she wanted to come for a swim. She wasn't keen but I eventually convinced her.

Down at the beach I took her over to Grampa Jack.

He said, 'I know you might be nervous going back in

the water, but we'll be watching all the time.'

And she said, 'I've got nothing to worry about. Nipper will be with me.'

Grampa looked at me and grinned. 'Don't forget to swim between the flags.'

After we swam, Mrs Kearsley thanked me for thinking of her. 'I didn't realise I needed to get back in the water. I'd lost my confidence. But I think I'm all right now.'

'Well, miss,' I said, 'you can't live at Bondi and not get wet.'

She laughed. 'Very true,' she said, 'but it helps when you've got a lifesaver right beside you.'

I didn't mind that she called me a lifesaver. I knew what she meant.

Wednesday, 23 February 1938

'Hey, Nipper. How you goin'?'

I had a nice chat with Arthur today. I was doing my grocery deliveries when he just popped up out of nowhere. Made me jump out of my skin.

I said hello. Then he helped me put the vegies back

in the box I'd been carrying.

'I see you been up that ceremony place.'

'Yeah, I was,' I said. 'But how do you know?'

'I'm not much of a tracker,' Arthur said, 'but you're not hard to track. Big Nipper school shoes. Then every few feet, kickin' something.'

I thought about the mood I'd been in. The ground must've been pretty scuffed.

'It looks like they're going to build something up there,' I said.

'Golf course,' he said. 'No more ceremonies up there, after. Not that there's any now. Pretty soon there won't be any place for old Arthur.'

'You gonna move?'

'Yeah, down that Lapa, maybe.'

'If you do, perhaps I could come visit?'

'If you not too busy bein' lifesaver?'

'You heard about that?'

'Yeah, I heard. Real good thing, what you did.'

'Thanks.'

'Reckon they'll give you that gold medal.'

'Bronze medallion. Nah. You have to be sixteen.'

'Yeah. That's the one. If you was in my tribe, we'd

give it to ya. Proper ceremony, everything.'

'Thanks,' I said, laughing, because I was pretty sure he was joking. 'There's nothing I can do but wait three more years.'

Arthur thought about that for a bit. Then he said, 'You want to know something, Nipper? You don't have to wait three years for them, they have to wait three years for you.'

Gee, that Arthur can make you feel good.

Sunday, 27 February 1938

The last weekend of summer proper, but it was really quiet on the beach. It was beautiful yesterday until a southerly buster came up. Sunny and warm one minute, then a line of big, dark clouds came racing up the coast. It went really still as the clouds came closer, then the wind hit and in minutes it was freezing cold and pouring with rain.

There were people and seagulls flyin' everywhere, as Grampa Jack says.

This morning it was still blowing cold from the south and the only people on the beach were the beachcombers. Ike Cole was down the southern end, this bloke named Banger was up our end. They were working towards each other, looking for things the wind and waves had uncovered – coins, jewellery, gold rings, false teeth. Those guys had eyes like hawks. Then down close to the water, Southerly Jack was walking on the edge of the surf looking for anything in the water glinting on the bottom. Lots of people have a go at beachcombing from time to time but those guys are at it all the time, whenever the conditions are right.

Well, Bondi Mary might be around from time to time too, but she wasn't that interested in finding treasures in the sea. She was usually on the lookout for food.

The breeze died off in the late afternoon, which meant it was beaut for the promenade. The last of the summer, although it would keep going on until it got too cold, in late autumn. There were lots of people walking up and down but you could feel that it was already becoming more locals than visitors. You can tell because there's a lot more people in groups talking than there are people just walking along.

I was with Mum and Dad when we came across Mrs Kearsley, who was walking on her own. As far as

I know, she doesn't usually promenade on Sunday evenings, but she did tonight. Mum and Dad stopped and chatted to her for ages, and of course they were saying nice things and she was saying nice things, which I have to admit was a bit of a change. Next thing I know, Mum and Dad invited Mrs Kearsley for fish and chips with us.

I was a bit, you'd have to say, horrified. So was Josie. Well, Mrs Kearsley's been a lot nicer since I saved her life, but we didn't want to have fish and chips with a teacher from school. Fish and chips are supposed to be fun. But then Mrs Kearsley smiled.

'That would be lovely,' she said.

You know what? Not even Mrs Kearsley can ruin fish and chips.

Thursday, 3 March 1938

That Bea Miles is something else. She was down on the beach today, swimming on her own.

Grampa Jack and I were on our usual walk home from the Diggers and we thought that the beach was deserted. There was a cold driving rain coming from the south, slab-grey chop breaking unevenly across the beach.

Then we noticed a woman was swimming down at the southern end. We went down there to see who it was.

'Guess who?' Grampa Jack said, 'It's Bea.'

She was out in the deeper water, catching big waves, and all around her there were dolphins catching the waves as well. Eventually she came out of the water, wrapped a towel around herself, then put on her coat and said, 'Oh, the water was beautiful. Did you see me out there with the dolphins?'

We said we did.

Then she walked up to the road and there was a taxi waiting there. It had been there all the time she was swimming. She got in and it drove off, back to where she lived, somewhere in Kings Cross.

Sunday, 6 March 1938

Mrs Kearsley was walking on the promenade again today. And she came for fish and chips after. It was actually pretty good. She really seems to enjoy it, and she was nice to me. Called me Nipper and everything. And me and Josie are allowed to call her Mrs K, but only outside school. Hope she doesn't find out she's got the same nickname as Jamie's horse.

She and Mum got along really well, especially when they were talking a lot about fundraising for the school. Like Mum doesn't have enough to do fundraising for the lifesavers.

Thursday, 10 March 1938

Hey diary. Wish me happy birthday. I'm thirteen. A teenager! In theory, I have to stay at school until the end of the year, but if I want to go now, no one can really stop me. Except, now it's not that simple. Mrs K would be pretty disappointed if I left. Mr Hester too. And Mum and Dad and Grampa Jack. And even Jamie.

We're having a birthday party on Saturday. Everyone who's coming is from school, or they're from my family. Mrs K is coming too. We sort of have this thing between us now. I mean I did save her life. It's funny. We kind of don't talk about it but every time we see each other, it's like being reminded of something that nobody else knows. She might put it better, but it's like, after you've saved someone's life, you realise they've only got one to lose. We've all only got one life, so don't waste it.

I got some more *Tarzan* books for presents and Rachel gave me a copy of *White Fang*, which is about a wolf. The best present of all, though, was this little key. Grampa Jack gave it to me.

'It's for the dinghy,' he said. 'I've been messing about in boats since I was your age. Reckon it's time I grew up. The dinghy's yours, but maybe you'll still take me out in it.'

So, thirteen. It seems growing up happens whether you like it or not. And the thing is, I could leave school, except Mr Hester is a really good teacher and it also makes a difference when all the other teachers are nice, especially Mrs K. She told me that if I needed any help, to ask her, but so far I haven't needed to. Besides, if there's something I don't understand, I can always ask Rachel. She's really smart.

Sunday, 20 March 1938

Grampa Jack invited me to a special event at the Bondi Lifesavers' club today.

'Put on your good clothes and meet me at the club at six-fifteen,' he said.

The afternoon patrol had finished putting away all the rescue gear but most of the other club members had assembled as well. They all went into the clubhouse, members only, but they let me in too.

The club president called for attention and then explained that the efforts of the club's members during Black Sunday had been recognised with a special certificate. He read it out.

'This certificate was awarded to the Bondi Lifesavers' Club for outstanding bravery on February 6, 1938.'

Then he said, 'For those who were there, this certificate will serve as a reminder.' Then he looked at me, 'For those who come after us, we hope it will serve as an inspiration.'

He talked some more about duty and service, and when he was finished, he recited the club motto: 'Ready, aye ready.'

Then the whole club, nearly three hundred-strong, responded, 'READY, AYE READY!'

The best part of all. They made me feel like I was one of them.

Monday, 21 March 1938

They were hauling up the shark net when Grampa Jack and I were walking home from the Diggers today. It looked like they caught about a dozen sharks, big ones and little ones. So if they're netting twice a week, that's maybe twenty sharks a week. Grampa Jack reckons, and so do I, that the nets are starting to make a difference. The shark fishermen on Sunday nights don't seem to be catching as many. Some blokes have given it away, knowing the nets are there. They reckon that when the nets get put in for the weekend and taken away on Monday, there's not much chance of catching a shark on Sunday night, when everyone is promenading.

Grampa Jack reckons shark fishing will soon be a thing of the past and I'm lucky I got to see it. I'm not sure if lucky is the right word. A lot of the time I feel sorry for the poor shark. They're scary and dangerous but seeing them all dead on the beach, I don't much enjoy seeing that. Not that seeing them dragged up in a net is any better.

Wednesday, 23 March 1938

Germany has invaded Austria. It's been in the newspapers, and Mum and Dad and the Freemans have been talking about it a lot. It sounds bad. Apparently, it means Hitler has broken the Treaty of Versailles, which was the rules Germany had to obey after the Great War. It could mean war, except the French Government is in too much of a mess to do anything and the British Government is trying to avoid confrontation. Except they don't call it that. The word they use is 'appeasement'. Every time anyone mentions it Mr Freeman gets quite upset.

'You should never give in to a bully,' he says.

Anyway, I've been doing those little sums again. If the war starts now, I'll be seventeen if it lasts for four years. Still not old enough. So maybe I'm in favour of appeasement, at least until 1939.

Saturday, 26 March 1938

I really don't want to write this down. But then, even if it's embarrassing, if you can't tell the truth in your diary, where can you? Still, it's hard but here goes.

You know how Rachel has been grumbling for

quite a while that girls are good enough to be lifesavers? So finally she said she'd prove it. She challenged me and Damo to a swimming race. To get your bronze medallion, you have to be able to swim four hundred yards. I knew I could do that. Damo reckoned he could too. So we said, 'Righto.'

The thing is, Rachel has been learning to swim with the Bondi Ladies Swimming Club and doing races with them most weekends. She's not that good, but while she's been doing that, Damo and I are usually just swimming around in the sea. It turns out that pool swimming isn't the same as ocean swimming. Anyway, long story short. She beat both of us by a lap. And we were exhausted. I mean, that distance, racing, is actually quite a long way. But Rachel was ready for more.

'Now,' she said, 'we tow someone fifty yards. I'll tow my mum, you tow yours.'

It turns out they practise that at the Bondi Ladies Swimming Club, especially since Black Sunday. In case someone needs help and there aren't enough lifesavers to go around. Well, I was already tired, so I struggled to drag Mum the length of the pool. By then Rachel was already out of the water, looking very pleased with herself.

And didn't she rub it in? As I dragged myself up the ladder she said, 'You all right, Nipper? You need Schafer Method?'

Apparently, most of the Ladies' Swimming Club can do that too.

Damo thought it was the funniest thing he'd ever seen.

Sunday, 10 April 1938

We've been learning a new word lately: reffos. It's short for refugees, and the strange thing is they're not trying to escape from the war. Rachel and her family are reffos, kind of, except it already feels like they've always been here. But ever since she got here, Mrs Freeman has been trying to get permits for friends and family to escape from Europe as well.

'She goes to the Immigration Department almost every day,' Rachel said, 'trying to convince them to give a permit for this one and that one.'

Since Austria got invaded, apparently lots more people are trying to leave.

Mum and Dad have been helping. Dad has been

giving guarantees whenever he can. He reckons that a lot of the people who are desperate to leave now, you couldn't have begged to leave only a year ago.

'Doctors, scientists, bankers,' he keeps saying as he shakes his head. 'The best minds in Europe, and a lot of them are coming here.'

You can't help noticing there are more and more reffos around Bondi. Some of them are opening new shops, others are going door to door selling that strange devon that reffos like. Sunday afternoons at Rachel's, it's wall-to-wall reffos. A lot of them don't have any family, or only a couple, so Rachel's parents have been gathering up the strays and putting on huge meals for everyone. It was like a party but a lot of people weren't very happy. Sometimes people would start crying and we soon learned not to ask why.

Saturday, 16 April 1938

Hey diary. Something different again today. We were all down at the beach when these big dark clouds started coming over from the west. There was no doubt we were in for a big storm, and everyone was ready to make a break for it when the rain came. But instead, hail. It hit about two in the afternoon while there were lots of people on the beach. There was no rain. It just came down hail and in a moment everyone was running for cover. It all came from just one big cloud. I'll never forget the way it looked: it was green, a big green cloud.

The Pavilion was soon packed with people, and those who couldn't get inside were trying to get under anything that gave them some cover. People were driving their cars under anything they could to protect them. You couldn't blame them. The hailstones were the size of cricket balls. Cars out in the open had their canvas hoods ripped to shreds. All the metal on them was dented and a lot of them had their windows smashed. It was the same with a lot of houses.

The hail only lasted ten minutes but there are still people cleaning up and we won't need a visit from the iceman for a few days. We gathered up lots of the hail and put it in the fridge for mum. She thought it was beaut.

Fortunately, no one seems to have been injured. There was lots of damage but everyone seemed to be able to get somewhere safe before they got hurt. Even the lifesavers were all right. Although there was a hailstorm, they had to stay on the beach. They got wooden fruit boxes, banana cases and so on, and used them as helmets to protect themselves.

Tuesday, 19 April 1938

Hey diary. I don't know if this is true or not but there's a story going around Bondi at the moment about a reverend gentleman who lost his teeth in the surf. He got hit by a wave and his false teeth flew out. They cost quite a bit of money, so up he goes to the lifesavers to see if they can help him find them.

They searched around, searched around. Nothing.

They told the reverend that they'd keep an eye out, and if they found his teeth would let him know. He was very grateful.

So then the lifesavers waited a couple of days before they got in contact and said they might have found his missing molars. Except they hadn't, really. They'd waited until this gentleman had gone back to his church, then they went and saw Southerly Jack.

'Found any false teeth lately, Southerly?' they asked.

'Find teeth all the time,' says Southerly. 'What kind

you lookin' for?' And out comes old Southerly with a box full of teeth. Loads of 'em.

So they picked out a few likely sets and called up His Worship.

'We found some teeth, but we're not sure if they're yours?'

The pastor came down, rummaged through the teeth, and he wasn't sure either.

'It would be a sin to take a set that aren't mine,' he said.

'Remember, Reverend,' the lifesavers replied, 'they've been tossed about in the sea, so they might not be exactly the same as they were. Why don't you try the most likely-looking set?'

And with that His Reverence found a set of teeth that were a perfect fit. Well, almost. He'd tried every pair in the box until he found some that were 'most satisfactory', then gave the lifesavers a pound and went on his way.

Monday, 25 April 1938

Today is Anzac Day, when we're supposed to remember those who fell in the service of their country. However, even though Grampa Jack is a Digger, he gets a bit funny about it every year. He doesn't march in the Anzac Day parade. He doesn't go to the dawn service or the wreath-laying at the war memorial. Most of his old war mates don't go either.

'But it's a day of remembrance,' I said to him when he told me he wasn't going.

'If you were there, young Nipper, you'd know it haunts you every bloody day of your life. Remembering ain't a problem. Forgettin'? That's the hard part.'

Instead, Grampa Jack and I went to the lifesaving club, where there's a plaque listing the club's members who served in the Great War and didn't come back. Then he went to the Diggers with his mates for lunch and I went back later for our walk home. We took a detour past the beach. The waves today were lazy. They were slowly lifting themselves out of a dead smooth sea, then flopping on to the sand like they were exhausted from the effort.

I like sitting with Grampa Jack on the wall of the promenade looking at the waves. It's one of my favourite things to do.

'You never talk about what happened in the war, Grampa Jack,' I said.

'No,' he replied. 'I don't.'

'But you got a medal for bravery,' I said. 'Everyone says you were a hero.'

'Well, you know what that's like,' he answered. 'Me? I was trying not to get killed and a few blokes got saved in the process.'

'I think I understand,' I said.

'I think you do too.'

We sat and watched the waves for a while longer, then Grampa Jack said, 'Brave young Nipper.'

And I said, 'Brave Grampa Jack.'

And we both just kind of looked at each other and smiled.

'Now that you've done it once,' Grampa Jack said, 'dived into the raging surf to save someone, would you do it again?'

I thought about how Mrs K had been at the end of her tether. Then how scared I'd been, fighting through the waves. And how tired I'd been dragging her back to the sand bank.

Then I thought about what might have happened if I'd done nothing.

'If I had to,' I finally said. 'I would.'

'Good answer. I like that you took your time to think about it. You'll make a good lifesaver one day.'

Sunday, 1 May 1938

There was plenty of fanfare down on the beach today. The Bondi club has taken delivery of a new surf boat. It was paid for with money the club raised after Black Sunday. Most of that was raised by the women in the club. They sure do have a knack for getting people to put their hands in their pockets to show their appreciation.

It's also finally dawned on me that Rachel wants to be a lifesaver as much as I do. And it really isn't fair. I mean, she's just like Damo and me except she's a girl. But there's all these lifesavers who reckon women aren't strong enough to handle heavy surf, let alone the reels and surfboats. Even so, if I couldn't be a lifesaver just because I was a girl, I'd absolutely hate it.

Mum doesn't think much of the rules either.

'Of course I'd like to be a lifesaver, although some of the blokes are a bit rough,' she said. 'Lifesaving is the only respectable thing some of them do.'

It turned out that they could ban women from being lifesavers but they couldn't stop them from saving lives. So down at the pool, the women swim, and they learn first aid like the Schafer method, and do all the things you have to do for the bronze medallion. They just aren't allowed to actually do the bronze medallion.

'You know why all you kids are allowed to come down here swimming on your own all the time?' Mum said.

I suspected she was going to tell me.

'We know that there's half a dozen mothers from the swimming club keeping an eye on you,' she said, 'often a closer eye than the lifesavers, because it's our kids in the water.'

And Grampa Jack agreed, 'We'd be stuffed without the women who support the club. I reckon they should be members. It doesn't matter who does the lifesaving as long as the person gets rescued.'

Tuesday, 3 May 1938

I think we might have started our own swimming club. Most mornings, down at the Bondi ocean pool, before school, Damo, Rachel and I go and swim laps, practising for our bronze medallion. The fact that Damo and I are still behind Rachel when it comes to swimming in a straight line might have a bit to do with it too. She thinks it's hilarious. And sometimes Mrs K comes and swims when she doesn't have to be at school early. She's joined the Ladies Swimming Club as well. Making the most of the one life each of us has. Even better, Grampa Jack sometimes comes down and coaches us.

Occasionally I'll go and swim a length of the beach on my own. I really do like being out in the waves. It's a bit more challenging, although I'm sure my technique has improved since I've been swimming with Rachel and Damo. I'm still not as fast as Bob Newbiggin but I like having something to aim for.

Wednesday, 4 May 1938

Grampa Jack is up to something. When I went to meet him at the Diggers, he wouldn't walk home with me.

'Sorry, Nip,' he said, 'I've got something special I need to attend to.'

Then he winked at me, like he had a secret.

He wouldn't say what it was. All he told me was that

the North Bondi surf club was having a meeting.

'We've got a bit of unfinished business from Black Sunday,' he said.

When I asked him what kind, he just acted all mysterious.

'All in good time, Nipper. All in good time.'

Thursday, 5 May 1938

Rachel was saying today that things are getting worse in Europe. Her mum got a permit for a family to come to Australia but when she tried to contact them they'd disappeared. No one knew where they'd gone. At the pictures on Saturday, the newsreels are often about what's happening. Although the war is still in Spain and China, there are people being assassinated and threats being made all the time. And when you see people like Hitler and Mussolini dressed in uniforms, shouting at these giant crowds, maybe war won't be so long in coming. Although when I look at the globe of the world in the living room, it all seems so far away. Watching the waves roll in at good old Bondi, one after the other, always different but always the same, it seems even further.

Friday, 6 May 1938

Grampa Jack is still acting strange. When I asked him how his meeting went, he just got this funny grin on his face.

Then he said, 'The club made a good decision. But I can't speak out of turn. There has to be an official announcement.'

I reckon they might be putting up a statue or something. Or maybe they're getting a new surf boat. Except, if it was something like that, Grampa Jack would at least give me a hint.

Saturday, 7 May 1938

We had one of those perfect autumn days today. Warm and sunny and no wind. The Freemans hosted a big gathering on the beach and people came from everywhere. All the reffos really stood out (except Mum and Dad reckon it's rude to call them that). Anyway, they all sat on the sand and took off their shoes and socks but none of them went swimming. Everyone was talking in their own languages – Polish, Hungarian, Austrian, German – or trying to talk in the little bit of English they knew. Dad and Mr Freeman and some other distinguished-looking gentlemen talked about bank stuff. Mum and Mrs Freeman and the other ladies laid out rugs and then started getting out all the salads and cold meats and stacked up all the bags full of cakes, ready for later. Us kids were given tin cups filled with lemonade. There was even a little stove for making those tiny cups of coffee that some reffos (sorry, Dad reckons they're *new Australians*) really like. We wanted to see how it worked but the man who owned it said we'd have to wait until people wanted coffee. He didn't want to waste fuel. So we all went walking on the beach, getting our legs wet, and a little bit of our clothes, when a wave caught some of the unwary kids, or the careless ones.

Then it was time for lunch. Back down the beach our parents were calling us. We went back to eat a huge meal. No way could we have a swim after eating so much, even though it was still warm enough. We'd have sunk for sure. So everyone sat on the shore of Bondi Beach while the man with the stove made little cups of coffee. Sometimes people walked past shaking their heads at such an assortment of new Aussies tossed up like flotsam after a storm, but no one paid them much attention. After a while, some people slept, some told stories, and everyone seemed happy, even the sad ones. When it came time to leave, no one wanted to go home. They wished this day could last forever. I wished I could tell them there'd be plenty more just like this. Everything else in the world might change but there would always be perfect days in the sun just sitting on the beach watching the waves roll in.

Wednesday, 11 May 1938

Hey diary. Big news today. I came home from school and there, in the hallway, was a telephone. It was a big brown wooden box attached to the wall with a wire coming out and going down to the floor. On the box was a dial for calling the operator, a big black mouthpiece for talking into, and a speaker on a cable that you could put to your ear to hear what the other person was saying. Mum was home and said not to touch it until Dad came home. So Josie and I, and Rachel and Damo, just stared at it. I didn't know why Mum and Dad decided to get a phone. Everyone we needed to talk to lived nearby. It was the same with cars. Some people had them, but most people walked or took the tram. Even when Rachel and Josie went to Girl Guides over in Bellevue Hill, they walked over there and then walked home around nine o'clock at night. Anyway, now Josie and I were racking our brains trying to think of who we could call. When Dad came home he pretended that the phone wasn't there!

'Dad,' we chorused, 'show us how it works.'

'Oh,' he said. 'I hadn't noticed we have a telephone.'

He kept teasing us until after we'd had our dinner. Then he said, 'Now, this telephone. Who do we know that we could call with it?'

We didn't know. Then he said, 'Well, what about your brother Jamie?'

We couldn't believe it was possible. Dad showed us how. He called the operator, asked for long distance and got put through to the phone at Uncle Neville's farm. And we got to talk to Jamie. He said he was happy I was still at school and he was doing good and he was proud of what I'd done on Black Sunday.

He couldn't talk for very long, because it's very expensive, but Mum and Dad reckon we can call him now, every couple of weeks, just to hear how he's getting along.

What a wonderful thing.

Friday, 13 May 1938

School holidays! It's great to have two weeks to muck around at home, but it feels a bit different now that I like school more. I don't mind that I'll be going back to funny old Mr Hester and his mental challenges and poems. For some kids though, it's the end of their schooling. And yeah, some kids might have been saying they were looking forward to the fun of no more school, but others were saying, 'Gotta leave. Me parents can't afford to keep me any longer.' That means every few months our little gang gets that little bit smaller.

Up on Ben Buckler, they've been doing work on the big disappearing gun. It's been up there since the 1890s but it hasn't been used for years. The disappearing gun is a nine-incher housed in a turret below ground level that uses its recoil to push itself back into the gun pit. Because it was only exposed when it was fired, and disappeared afterwards, it was almost impossible for enemy ships to hit. There were more modern guns up on the heads of Sydney Harbour, but the Ben Buckler gun was held 'in reserve' in case it was needed if war came.

And it looks like it might be coming. All around Bondi you can see bomb shelters being started in private homes and public parks. At school there was talk of doing air-raid drills, but no one did anything.

Anyway, today, the army did a letterbox drop warning that there would be a test firing of the disappearing gun next Monday at noon. They said that there would be quite a bit of noise but no danger to the public. A spectator area was being set aside for anyone who wanted to view the firing.

Monday, 16 May 1938

Most of Bondi went to see the firing of the disappearing gun, or rather hear it. The viewing area was well away from the gun itself, for safety, and the gun is set into the hill anyway. So we all waited patiently, then at twelve there was a massive *BOOM!* and a puff of smoke from behind some heath. I guess it works, 'cause we never actually saw the disappearing gun. Then, right out at sea, a couple of miles, there was a splash when the shell hit the water. You couldn't hear the splash because of all the neighbourhood dogs barking.

We were walking back down the hill when we came across Arthur. He'd been watching the gun too. He was carrying a big bag full of clothes and bits and pieces. Rachel, Damo and I said hello. Arthur said hello back.

'You goin' somewhere?' Damo asked.

'Lapa,' he said. 'All them seaplanes roaring up and down Rose Bay bad enough. Now they got this big gun. Ain't no peace round here no more.'

'We'll miss you,' I volunteered. 'Maybe we could come and visit.'

'Or I'll visit you,' he said. 'I'll still be around, keeping an eye on things.'

'Please do, Arthur,' Rachel said.

'Me too,' I said. 'Bondi won't be the same without you.'

'No,' he said sadly. 'It won't.'

The others said goodbye and followed all the other kids. But I lingered with Arthur. There was something I wanted to tell him.

'Arthur,' I began. 'You remember telling me that I wouldn't have to wait to be a lifesaver?'

'Yeah, I remember that.'

'Arthur,' I said. 'I just wanted to say thank you. It made me look at things a lot differently.'

'Aah,' he said, and he looked at me for a moment. 'You're very welcome, young man.'

He reached out and shook my hand. Then he went on his way and I ran to catch up with the others.

Tuesday, 17 May 1938

Hey diary! You'll never believe what just happened.

There was a letter waiting for me when I got home today. It's not like I get a letter very often, so I didn't realise it was there until Mum pointed it out to me.

'I think there might be something for you on the mantelpiece,' she said.

It was from the North Bondi Life Saving Club, addressed to Master David McCutcheon. I was going to take it to the sleepout and read it but Mum insisted I sit on the lounge with her while I opened it. Here's what it said:

Dear David,

As President of the North Bondi Surf Life Saving Club it is my pleasure to inform you that at a recent special club meeting our members considered a motion to offer you an honorary surf life saver membership. The motion was proposed in recognition of your valiant efforts on Black Sunday. The motion was passed unanimously.

Your honorary membership will remain valid until you are sixteen and eligible to qualify for your Bronze Medallion and full membership. May I take this opportunity to offer you my heartfelt congratulations and I hope this honour marks the beginning of an association with our great club that will extend many, many years into the future.

A small ceremony is being organised for Saturday, 21 May at 5 pm in the clubrooms, at which your membership certificate will be presented. Please indicate your availability to attend at your earliest convenience.

Yours sincerely …

'Mum,' I said, 'They want to make me a lifesaver.'

She was crying as she gave me a big hug.

Later, at the Diggers, I reckon Grampa Jack might have shed a tear too.

As for me, I don't think it's possible for anyone to be as happy as I am now.

Saturday, 21 May 1938

Everyone I know turned up for the presentation ceremony at the club. Even Jamie and Uncle Neville and Auntie May came down. All the club officials were there in their blazers. It was standing room only and I was so shy I was glad I didn't have to say anything, although I was squirming in the centre of attention.

Then the President made a little speech. I can't remember all of it but there's one thing I can remember clearly. He said: 'There are many qualities that make a good lifesaver but there's one that stands above all others. We are volunteers. When we face danger, we do so by choice, seeking nothing in return. On Black Sunday young David McCutcheon demonstrated the strength of character that is the essence of what it means to be a lifesaver. It is my honour to present him with this certificate of membership.'

Then there was applause and everyone shook my hand and patted me on the back. My head was nearly spinning from all the attention. Know what, though? I kind of liked it.

While we were at the club there was quite a bit of talk about a new section that they're thinking of setting up for aspiring lifesavers like me. It would get them involved and give them some training for when they're eligible for the bronze medallion. I thought it was a great idea. I'd certainly join. Most kids in Bondi would too.

When I got home, I hung my certificate next to the poster of the lifesaver. Grampa Jack helped me put it up while everyone else watched.

'Proud of you, Nip,' he said. 'Proud as proud.'

Sunday, 22 May 1938

Sunday promenade, one of the last of this summer, and everyone in Bondi had heard I was made an honorary lifesaver. We barely moved along the concourse, there was so much handshaking and congratulating to get through.

It was getting a bit much, but then Dad said, 'All your friends are really happy for you.'

He was right. They were. After that, I was a lot happier too.

Mind you, I was glad when we went for fish and chips. There was us, and Damo and his family and Rachel and her parents and Mrs K, of course, all having a great meal, sitting on a bench or around it.

We'd been sitting there for a while when I said, 'Dad, do you think there's going to be a war?'

Just asking the question, you could feel everyone become a little tense.

'Unfortunately, Nipper, yes,' he said. 'Everywhere you look, people are getting ready. Even at the bank, Rachel's dad and I have been planning how we'll operate on a wartime footing. In all kinds of areas, people are doing the same thing.'

'Do you know when it might start?'

'Well, probably not tomorrow,' he said, 'But within two years, most likely.'

'Why do you ask?' Mrs K enquired.

'Well,' I said, 'I've been doing some calculating. If the war starts soon, and lots of lifesavers join up, they'll be short of patrol members by the summer of 1940–41. I turn sixteen in March 1941, but if they're short, they might take me that summer rather than the one after.'

'That figures,' Dad said. 'But what if you left school

and were working somewhere else? That might change things.'

'No, Dad. I have to stay at school as long as I can.'

'This is news,' Mum said.

'Well,' I said, 'it's like this. I want to be a lifesaver and, like you say, if I leave school that might make things difficult, like what happened to Jamie. But I'm starting to think that school might not be such a bad idea either.'

'What's brought this about?' Dad enquired.

'Lots of things, but for a start, I've got nice teachers,' I said, and I think Mrs K might have blushed. 'And if it hadn't been for Mrs K getting us to write diaries, I might not have found out how much I like writing. So I reckon, if I stay at school a bit longer, who knows what other things I might find out I like?'

Mum and Dad and Mrs K laughed at that.

'Nipper,' Mrs K said, 'You'd be amazed.'

Monday, 23 May 1938

'Rachel,' I whispered. 'You awake, Rachel? C'mon, they're bitin'.'

There was a complaining sort of moan from inside

her bedroom. She said something about it being only five o'clock.

'Come on, sleepy,' I said. 'You said you wanted to come.'

This morning, I took Rachel fishing instead of Grampa Jack. He reckoned she might enjoy it. And he wasn't wrong. She wasn't real keen when it came to actually going but after we got the dinghy in the water and started rowing out over the gently rising swells, and she felt safe, she started to come good. When we caught two bream and a small flathead, she was really enjoying it.

And then the day came. The clouds were deep red, then orange and pink and mauve. The sky went from deepest blue to daylight in just a few minutes. Then the sea kicked up a bit of mist that shone gold in the first rays of the rising sun. One of those wonderful Bondi mornings.

'Behold,' I said, like I'd magically made it happen.

'Oh, Nipper,' she sighed, 'it's so beautiful.'

Rachel was good in the boat too. She understood how to stay in the middle and we only came close to tipping once, but that was more the fault of the flathead we caught. Rachel jumped back to avoid the barb it has and if I hadn't jumped the other way, we'd have been swimming.

When she came home with three good fish, her mum reckoned Rachel could come fishing any time.

Wednesday, 1 June 1938

Winter has come again. Bondi is back to being a little seaside town where you know everyone you see. Kids, teachers (yeah, back to school again this week), lifesavers, Mr Smith the greengrocer, the iceman, Southerly Jack and Bondi Mary. But alas, no Arthur.

It's getting too cold for most people to swim, although Rachel, Damo and I are still doing a few laps. We've got a bit of a routine going there now.

So while Bondi has changed into its winter ways, other things have stayed the same. Like school, walking home with Grampa Jack, going fishing. And of course the beach doesn't change. There are new buildings going up, and maybe a war is coming, but the waves just keep breaking in a line across the beach, then slapping into the wet sand, chasing the gulls and the beachcombers up the shore.

Friday, 3 June 1938

Hey diary. Happy birthday. I've been writing in you for twelve months exactly, so now you're one year old. It's amazing how much I've written. Especially when I read how much I didn't want to write a diary when I started. I'm really glad I did but.

I can't believe how much has happened. For starters, a year ago Mrs K and I were enemies. Well, maybe not enemies, but we didn't get along. And now she's not my teacher any more but she's like a friend of our whole family. And I saved her life. That's something neither of us will forget in a hurry.

As for being a lifesaver, I still want to do that more than anything. The thing is, the reasons I want to be a lifesaver have changed. It's hard to explain. It's like, when I was just a kid, I wanted to be a lifesaver because I thought it would make me a hero. Now that I'm more grown up, and an honorary lifesaver, I don't want to be a hero, but I still want to be a lifesaver.

I reckon Black Sunday has a lot to do with that. It's not just because of what happened to me, it's mostly because I found out what it really means to be a lifesaver. They call it Black Sunday because of the loss of life but it was also one of Bondi's finest hours. When hundreds of people were panicking and struggling and in danger in the surf, nearly a hundred others, men and women, were running and diving and swimming into danger to help them. I'll never forget such courage as long as I live.

I still have my poster from the sesquicentenary celebrations over my bed, showing a lifesaver looking out to sea, ready for anything. Who knows what the future might bring but I hope I have the courage to be like him. Ready for anything. Ready, aye ready.

Historical Notes

For narrative purposes, some licence has been taken with aspects of this story. In particular, 'Ready, aye ready' is the motto of the North Bondi Life Saving Club. Here it is used as the motto of lifesaving clubs generally.

The aircraft that arrived in Sydney on Christmas Eve 1937 was an Empire flying boat on a reconnaissance flight from England prior to the establishment of a regular commercial service between Europe and Australia. Catalina flying boats, which were involved in military operations, did not become a regular sight in Sydney until the Second World War. In modern times a restaurant in Rose Bay called Catalina's recognises their connection with the Rose Bay Seaplane Base, as detailed in the historical notes. Float planes still operate from the bay.

The Bondi Diggers Club was established in 1947. Bondi Golf Club, on the headland at North Bondi, was established in 1935. The golf club and Diggers combined in 2000, and both are now accommodated in the golf club's premises.

Black Sunday is the largest mass rescue on any Australian beach and one of the largest mass rescues in Australian history. It's estimated that on 6 February 1938 between 200 and 300 swimmers were swept into deep water at Bondi Beach and between 70 and 100 lifesavers and members of the public were involved in efforts to bring them to shore. It's believed that around 40 of those rescued were unconscious when taken from the water and all but four were able to be revived. One of those who died, Charles 'Sweety' Sauer, drowned while trying to save the life of a young girl. The death toll rose to five when the body of Michael Taylor was washed ashore four days later.

Among the rescuers, beltman George Pinkerton was dragged under when well-meaning members of the public pulled too hard on his line and he required resuscitation when he reached the beach. Another beltman is reputed to have rescued 25 people using his belt and line. A 16-year-old member of the Bondi Amateur Swimming Club, Ted Lever, was co-opted to be a beltman because he was known to be a strong swimmer. After Black Sunday, he was made an honorary member of the Bondi Surf Bathers' Life Saving Club until he completed his bronze medallion and became a full member.

The **surf-o-planes** (small inflatable craft – the forerunner of modern boogie boards – invented just a few years earlier by Dr Ernest Smithers) were both the heroes and villains of Black Sunday. They gave many of those swept into the sea something to help them stay afloat, and the actions of the staff at Stan McDonald's surf-o-plane hire in bringing more surf-o-planes to the beach during the emergency probably helped save many lives. However, it is likely that surf-o-planes contributed to the number of people who were endangered, as they gave weaker swimmers unjustified confidence in their ability to cope with the conditions in the surf.

Surf-o-planes are considered by some in the surfing community as having contributed greatly to Australia's surf culture. Many top surfers of the 1960s and 1970s learned the skills for catching waves on surf-o-planes before progressing to surfboards.

Bondi's two **piers** were built during the 1930s and allowed people to walk down tunnels from the male and female changing rooms near the Pavilion directly on to the beach. The concrete piers were demolished in 1942 owing to fears they could provide cover if there was an enemy invasion of the beach. Unfortunately, there was a miscalculation of the amount of dynamite required to do the demolition job, and shop fronts along Campbell Parade were damaged by flying debris.

The Bondi Surf Bathers' Life Saving Club claims to be the oldest **lifesaving club** in the world. It was established on 21 February 1907 at the Royal Hotel, Bondi Beach. Many other lifesaving clubs formed at or about the same time. Manly had formed a Surf and Life Saving Club in 1903 but it wasn't until 1911 that it split into the Manly

Life Saving Club and the Manly Surf Club. Some records suggest that Bronte Surf Lifesaving Club was also formed as early as 1903. North Bondi Surf Life Saving Club claims to have been formed as the North Bondi Surf and Social Club in January 1907, a month before Bondi (the North Bondi club's website claims 1906). What is beyond argument is that the Bondi club pioneered lifesaving, in particular the use of surf belts and reels.

In October 1907 a number of clubs met and formed the Surf Bathing Association of New South Wales, which eventually became Surf Life Saving Australia. Red and yellow flags were introduced in 1935, separated diagonally, rather than horizontally. Before then, patrol flags were blue and white. The flags were originally only used on beaches but have since become used throughout Australia to indicate safe/patrolled swimming areas.

In 2007 Australia celebrated the Year of the Surf Lifesaver.

The first **surf rescues** were performed using a lifebuoy and rope until the first surf belts and reels appeared on Sydney beaches in 1907. Lifesaver Lyster Ormsby and a soldier, Warrant Officer John Bond, devised the first belt and reel by making a small model using a cotton reel and two hairpins. A local coachbuilder then produced a full-sized reel made from wood. A handle allowed the reel to be wound and unwound, with a brake mechanism added not long after. The line was waxed to make it waterproof, and therefore lighter and less likely to tangle. Modern synthetic lines don't require waxing, although some belt and line competitors continue the practice.

The first **surf belts** were made from cork, and the idea was that the beltman would swim the belt to the patient, put it on the patient and then swim back with the patient, reassuring them as they went. This proved unwieldy, and swimming in the belt was difficult. The line could also become tangled in the belt. In one instance, a tangle caused a lifesaver to be drowned. Modified belts with fewer corks and quick release mechanisms were devised and rescues were carried out with the lifesaver remaining in the belt, supporting the patient as they were both pulled ashore. Two more deaths in 1950 led to the design of the Ross safety belt, which became the standard lifesaving belt.

In 1957 the first powered craft were tested for rescues on Queensland beaches. Jet boats and inflatable boats were tested in 1960. Rescues using helicopters were also investigated.

The **Bondi Icebergs** Swimming Club was established in 1929, its venue an ocean pool at the southern end of Bondi. It is one of many winter swimming clubs around Australia including the Cronulla Polar Bears, Clovelly Eskimos, Maroubra Seals, Coogee Penguins, Wollongong Whales and Cottesloe Crabs.

For many years the Surf Life Saving Association believed that **women** were not strong enough to operate the equipment involved in rescues or to swim in heavy surf. They were banned from qualifying for the bronze medallion, which was a requirement for anyone doing surf patrols.

At some clubs women became involved anyway: some worked in administration and fundraising, some formed ladies' surf clubs. Outside major cities, where the number of volunteer lifesavers was limited, the rules were less strictly followed, and women could be seen competing at surf carnivals.

As surf-rescue techniques evolved, in particular the use of inflatable rescue boats (often called IRBs), the argument that women weren't strong enough to perform rescues lost what little credibility it had. In 1980 women were admitted as full members by the Surf Life Saving Association. While an old guard in lifesaving remained sceptical and discriminatory, since 1980 the inclusion of women has seen the number of active lifesavers almost double.

Various junior lifesaving programs were run by some clubs as early as the 1920s and 1930s. They were often referred to as **'Nippers'** and aimed at boys (and sometimes girls) aged five to 13. It was not until the 1960s that the Surf Life Saving Association established a national Nippers program, in part to address falling membership, which threatened the future of some clubs. The early success of Nippers grew after 1980 when girls were also allowed to participate. As of 2015, there were more than 60,000 children involved in Nippers, while senior lifesavers number just over 100,000.

'Ready, aye ready' is the motto of the North Bondi Life Saving Club. It is also the motto of the Canadian Navy. 'Aye ready' is also associated with the Edinburgh Fire Brigade, the world's oldest, established in 1824. In the text, for narrative purposes, I've used the motto interchangeably with Bondi Life Saving Club.

Shark nets were first deployed at locations along the New South Wales coast in the 1930s and at several popular Sydney beaches, including Bondi, from 1937 onwards. They are still used today although their use remains a source of concern over their impact on the marine environment. Supporters of netting point to the fact that there hasn't been a fatal shark attack at Bondi since netting began, although it appears that shark attacks at Bondi were already extremely rare in the decades before they were used. Meanwhile, opponents of netting highlight all the other marine creatures that are also killed in the nets, particularly dolphins and turtles.

Beatrice (Bea) Miles (1902–73) is one of Sydney's best known and most colourful eccentrics. Highly intelligent, well educated but unapologetically unconventional, she was committed to a mental asylum by her father in her early years. Upon her release she resumed a bohemian lifestyle and gained a reputation for frequently taking taxis and avoiding paying the fare. However, on one occasion in 1955, she took a taxi to Perth, Western Australia, and paid her way there and back, a sum of £600. She read several books a week until she was banned from the Library of New South Wales in the late 1950s. She was arrested by police innumerable times for a wide range of misdemeanours, and claimed she'd been 'falsely convicted 195 times, fairly 100 times'.

New Zealander **Ena Stockley** (1907–89) was a champion swimmer who was present at Bondi during the events of Black Sunday. She was involved in multiple rescues, demonstrating that women were entirely capable of being lifesavers despite the opinions of lifesaving authorities at the time.

Ena was New Zealand's 22nd Olympian, competing in the 1928 Olympic Games in the 100 yard freestyle and 100 yard backstroke.

Born and raised in Newcastle, New South Wales, **Bob 'Newbo' Newbiggin** (1921–89) is considered the greatest surf swimmer in the history of the sport. At an early age he was recognised for his ability in both ocean swimming and still-water events. At the age of 15 he held every national junior swimming record and was claimed to be the fastest schoolboy swimmer in the world. However, his passion was surf swimming and after placing fifth in the 1938 British Empire Games (aged 17) he focused his attention on surf competitions. He won the Australian junior surf and belt titles twice, in 1937–8 and 1938–39. He won the senior surf championship in 1939–40. During the war, he became a flight lieutenant with the RAAF and flew over 30 missions in heavy bombers over Germany. After the war, he won the senior surf championship in 1945–6, 1946–7, and 1947–8. He then concentrated on his career and married life but remained active in the surf lifesaving movement, as President of Nobby's Beach Life Saving Club; founding member, first captain and chief instructor of Tasmania's first lifesaving club, Hobart-Carlton; and at Manly in Queensland and Ballina in northern New South Wales. He is an inductee to the Sport Australia Hall of Fame and the Surf Lifesaving Association Hall of Fame.

Aub Laidlaw (1909–92) was a long-time Bondi resident and a beach inspector/lifeguard from the 1930s until the 1970s. He was a champion swimmer who made the Olympic swimming team in 1928 but didn't attend the games because the team was underfunded. He was a beach inspector and present at Bondi during the events of Black Sunday.

In later years he gained notoriety while enforcing Waverley Council's regulations on bathing costumes. He became famous for using a tape measure to check that women's bikinis were not too small. Much of the background material for this book was sourced from transcripts of oral history recordings made by Aub in 1989, and held by Waverley Council.

Bondi Mary (1870–1941) was a vagabond who frequented the Bondi area for almost a decade until she was found dead in a cave near the beach in 1941. She was a solitary figure, usually wearing sandshoes and an army greatcoat over ragged clothing, and living on scraps scavenged from garbage bins.

Little was known about her background until her death, from 'malnutrition and senile decay', at which time it was discovered that she had a son who was a Sydney businessman with a young family. He revealed that, years before, Bondi Mary had been a sought-after dressmaker trading as 'Madame Jacquier, French Modiste'. However, in 1913, when her son was aged nine, there was a violent gas explosion in his mother's flat in Milson's Point and the force of the blast threw her through the roof, with severe burns. The son recovered, but his mother suffered a brain injury and was later admitted to a mental hospital. After her release his family struggled to induce her to stay with them but apart from occasional visits, she became a recluse, living in her cave at Bondi, coming to be known as Bondi Mary.

In early 1937 Australia agreed to become part of the Empire Air Mail Scheme, which would see large aircraft fly regular mail and passenger services between England and New Zealand and numerous British Empire destinations along the way, including Australia. The aircraft were to be of such a size that there were few airfields along the route where they could land, so the idea was to use large flying boats that could land on sheltered waters virtually anywhere. **Rose Bay**, on Sydney Harbour, was chosen as the most suitable landing place for the **Sydney Air Mail base**, and constructions of hangars, slipways and terminal facilities were begun.

The first flying boat, a Short S23 Empire flying boat named *Centaur*, arrived in Sydney on a reconnaissance flight on Christmas Eve, 1937. The first regular service commenced in July 1938, operated by Imperial Airways and Qantas Empire Airways and became known as the Kangaroo Route.

Resuscitation techniques

Over the last 250 years, there have been a number of techniques devised for reviving people who had stopped breathing or whose heart had stopped beating.

In the twentieth century, Australian lifesaving clubs initially adopted the Schafer method devised by English physiologist Sir Edward Albert Sharpey-Schafer (1850–1935). This involved performing chest compressions on a patient positioned face down. Its effectiveness may have been questionable but it should be noted that some 40 unconscious patients were treated using this method during Black Sunday, and 36 of them recovered.

In 1952 the Holger Nielsen method devised by Danish fitness instructor Colonel Holger Louis Nielsen (1866–1955) became the preferred resuscitation method for Australian lifesavers to use. In essence it was an improved form of the Schafer method.

Expired Air Resuscitation (using mouth-to-mouth and chest compressions) was adopted in 1960. This method, now known as cardio-pulmonary resuscitation (CPR), has undergone refinement over the following years and now includes a method that allows the use of hands only in case the person attempting the resuscitation is unwilling or unable to perform mouth-to-mouth.

The current technique is outlined by the letters DRSABCD, which stands for Danger, Response, Send for Help, Airway, Breathing, CPR and Defibrillator, as detailed below:

DRSABCD

Danger	make sure you, the patient and others aren't in danger
Response	check for a response to speech and touch
Send for help	dial 000
Airway	Make sure it's not blocked
Breathing	Check that the patient isn't breathing. If they aren't, commence resuscitation
CPR	30 chest compressions, then 2 breaths. Alternatively, just perform chest compressions. Breaths are more important for drowning victims. Ideally, chest compressions should be at the rate of 100 compressions per minute, about the speed of the beat in the Bee Gees song 'Stayin' Alive'.
Defibrillator	continue CPR until a defibrillator can be employed

It's worth noting that even if you're not sure of what you're doing, it's better to attempt CPR than not to do CPR.